As a life-long lover of literature and writing, J James has dedicated his career to educating students, helping them develop the tools they'll need to share their stories in the future. After almost two decades in teaching and educational leadership, J James released his debut novel, *Denial Deceit Discovery*, which was a deeply personal story written as a way to reconcile parts of his own life. Four years later and J James has returned with a fictional novel titled *Happy Never After*.

James currently lives and works in Southeast Asia. He enjoys the tropical climate and the relaxed pace, which has provided the perfect opportunity to continue developing ideas for his writing.

Dedication

Dedicated to the loving memory of Antonio – my wonderful grandfather and best friend. Always and forever. x

J James

HAPPY NEVER AFTER

AUSTIN MACAULEY PUBLISHERS™

LONDON • CAMBRIDGE • NEW YORK • SHARJAH

A CIP catalogue record for this title is available from the British Library.

ISBN 9781528905596 (Paperback)
ISBN 9781528905602 (E-Book)

www.austinmacauley.com

First Published (2018)
Austin Macauley Publishers Ltd™
25 Canada Square
Canary Wharf
London
E14 5LQ

Acknowledgements

When I started writing my first book, *Denial Deceit Discovery*, I never imagined to see it on the shelves of a bookstore. To now have a second book is a blessing and I am very grateful to those who have supported me and helped me to keep going when I doubted myself. A special 'thank you' to Rochelle Weinstein, a fellow author who taught me the meaning of 'pay it forward'. You truly define this phrase, Rochelle. You have supported me for many years now and given me a push when I have felt less positive about the direction of my work. I cannot express my gratitude enough. I never would have realised this dream had it not been for you. One day in Miami, I hope.

Thank you to everyone at AM Publishing for their support and professionalism and for always being so patient with my constant questions. Special thank you to Amy Berger – the most positive editor in the world, who has always believed in this book and challenged me to push myself to write better and to have confidence in the work I produce. Thank you to Ana Grigoriu-Voicu for the amazing book cover. Despite my unclear brief, the cover is beyond my expectations and I am lucky to have had you share your creativity with me.

The greatest reward from writing my *Denial Deceit Discovery* was connecting with readers, particularly those who found comfort in the contents of the book. Readers from all over the world continue to make contact with me and this provides such a purpose for my writing. I am so grateful for the love shown and I really hope you enjoy *Happy Never After* as much.

Final thanks goes to the people whose love, support and encouragement have enabled me to do what I love to do. To friends and family who have supported me from the first ideas of book one until now – thank you! Special thanks to Fiona, Eileen and Bobby for their encouragement and for always making the time to read the book as it was unfolding. Writing is about passion and love and it is because of the love of my husband, Tommy, that I am able to bring this to my books. *Selalu dan selamanya!*

Chapter One

It's the same routine every Saturday morning. I roll over to nestle into Max to find that he hasn't come home from his usual Friday night fuck frenzy. Of course, I am not as stupid as Max presumes and I know exactly what is going on. But I am scared. Scared of being alone. Scared of putting myself back out there. Max is my security blanket – financially and emotionally. I need him. There is always the hope that one day *he* will need me as much as I need him. *Get real, kid.* My inner voice seems to have already given up on this loser.

I throw myself under the luxury cotton sheets Max insisted we purchase and tearfully ponder on his words before he swaggered out of the apartment the previous evening. Max is incredibly suave and impossibly handsome. And, of course, he knows this. As the false promises came dancing out of his perfectly sculptured mouth last night, I briefly believed that Max could change. 'Hey, babe, don't look at me like that. I will be back by midnight. I promise. It's just a work thing.' I had not even bothered to wait up to see if Max would keep his word. After one year of hearing similar speeches, it has grown somewhat tiresome. *Yet, you never fail to be sucked back in, time after time.*

The bright sunlight beams through the over-sized windows in our riverside penthouse and cascades across the four walls of the bedroom, making it difficult for me to drift back off to sleep, and forcing me to face up to the cold, hard fact – This. Relationship. Is. Over. Of course, three years ago, when Max had first mesmerised me with his fudge brown eyes, the future seemed so promising. I still recall the excitement of the first time we met. He walked into the room, commanding the attention of everyone in a way that only Max can. It is not so much the words he uses but his presence. The perfect blend of the cheeky London chap, and the charm and class of high society. I was 25 and a classic rich-kid bum. Jobless, university drop-out and perpetual traveller, following my gap year travels to Asia. I can see myself now – second row from the front as Max took to the stage. Key note speaker on *"Success is not a dream"*. It was my father's idea that I attend: a condition of me continuing to receive a monthly allowance and possibly a desperate hope that it may actually inspire me.

On two occasions, I was sure Max's stare had lingered in my direction. Or maybe that was just me hoping, since I knew deep down, I could never attract a guy like him. I was already undressing him in my mind. It was the way his shirt wrapped itself tightly around his rounded shoulders and accentuated his broad chest. Honestly, I took no notice of the message in his lecture but I did intensely observe his lips wrap around each word. Upper and lower lips perfectly balanced, and framed with a one day stubble. At the end of the session, I hung around like a silly high school girl waiting to carry the teacher's books. Fifteen minutes of small talk and finally, Mr Henderson asked me out for a drink. He was so incredibly attentive that first night and his eyes remained fixated on me throughout. And that charm! God that bloody innate charm he possesses wooed me into bed on the first night. *Whore!* I could not resist and that inability to resist kept me coming back night after night until before I knew it, I was in so deep. Truly swept right off my feet and it felt incredible. I thought I had found my soulmate: my other half. I admired him so much. He was my older man who looked after me and treated me like a rare precious stone, held ever so gently in his hand.

Reflecting back hurts. I cannot understand why things changed. Max was so romantic in the beginning. Forever showering me with gifts. Always making time for me. *You are doing it again, Robbie. Fooling yourself it was all roses and sun rays.* Deep down, I guess, I knew Max was a compulsive liar and maybe I even knew he was sleeping around. Yet, I chose to ignore it. And why? Because I am weak maybe? I was in love with the idea of being in love and I have the most amazing ability to conjure up a reality that is based on the unreal. People become characters that in my mind I can change and situations I find myself in become malleable. And all in the name of LOVE.

I had grown up in difficult circumstances, with little love and minimal attention. Max provided a sense of normality for me in a world where I had only ever known dysfunctional relationships in my family and even with my own past lovers, I guess. An only child, my parents were too busy arguing over my father's persistent infidelity to even notice I had grown up. And now, here I am. Living my mother's life. Suffering the same emotional and mental torture that she has endured for twenty-something years. In fact, the similarities are unnerving. My father is a rich CEO and Max, a successful entrepreneur. Both are certified Playboys and compulsive cheats. My *darling* mother is a frustrated housewife and although I am not quite playing *that* role, I am an unemployed web designer, dependent on the money brought to the table by my partner. I am grateful for this. It was Max's money that had paid my escalating tuition fees when I returned to Uni as a mature student. *Can you believe they referred to me as mature at just 27?* And it is the same source of funding that has provided the high-class lifestyle we both now enjoy in the vibrant city of London, although, my father insists on depositing random amounts into my account only to find I have returned the money a few days later. I need his attention now, not his money, but he fails to recognise that or does not care. For four years, I was living the dream – a dream in the sense that my eyes were closed to the realisation that I was in an open relationship without even knowing it. Yet, for the last six months since graduating from London Metropolitan in 2013, things have felt somewhat different.

'Robbie, where are you babe?' bellows Max, shouting up the long corridor as the over-sized entrance door slams shut behind him. The dirty dog is back and clearly, his tail is not between his legs. I can't face another single lie so I spring from the bed, and throw on the nearest pants and sweater, stomp down the hallway straight past Max and out through the door into the January morning air that never fails to bite.

Chapter Two

The warm blast from the over-door heater provides a welcome relief as I step inside the quaint coffee house that sits nestled amongst an array of intriguing boutiques and food outlets in the centre of Soho. The presence of Christmas decorations still in residence puzzle me slightly. Clearly, the new owners do not know the Twelve days of Christmas rule. Sitting in the corner in her usual outrageous fashion is Kimberly Jones – the perfect fag-hag for any gay. With no man of her own to please, she is readily available to entertain my latest West End show. Ever since Kimberly and I met one drunken evening way back, the drama that is our lives has never failed to keep the conversation flowing. *I think you will find it is more one-sided.* Admittedly, my stories were usually long and the emotions amplified but Kimberly cannot help but pity me. I was just a regular guy looking for a stable relationship yet now so blinded by love, *you mean the lifestyle,* I accept a compromised form of the relationship with Max.

'Bloody hell, it's just got hot in here!' screeches Kimberly desperately trying to stir some life into me as I mope towards her. Her bosoms are on show as usual as she knows these are her key weapons of attraction. Her skin glows the usual shade of orange, and the copper hair and lashes are overly large. Despite being a larger lady, Kimberly is confident and comfortable in her skin.

'Oh someone got a spray tan this morning,' I tease.

'Robbie, you are such a bitch,' she chuckles as she throws her arms around me. 'So what's *he* done now then?'

The prime location of the local coffee shop provides one of the best people-watching opportunities in London. Every possible representative of the gay world is sure to pass-by over the next hour or two. The macho gym boys, the effeminate slim guys and the inter-racial couples. It is a welcomed distraction from my woes and provides the opportunity to make the occasional bitchy comment as the crowds trundle past. 'Oh my God, what the hell is he wearing,' giggles Kimberly as the rather tall and incredibly slim European guy, sporting a pair of rather skimpy denim shorts and heeled shoes, steps inside, and gives a little wave.

'Now why can't you consider a nice young man like him?' giggles Kimberly. I find humour in her comment yet sense my bottom lip droop, right on cue whenever I feel overwhelmed or upset, especially when it comes to Max.

'Rob, haven't we been here many times before?' asks Kimberly with a little more sympathy. 'You know what you are getting with Max. A cheat and a liar. If...'

'Hey, you don't know that for sure,' I interrupt, always quick to defend Max. I can handle being the one talking badly of Max but was not ready to allow anyone else to do it.

'Oh, Robbie, get real! You caught the guy in bed with... what was his name?'

'Adam. His name is Adam and he is Max's business partner, remember?' I snap defensively.

'Oh yeah, *business* partner. It's common practice in these parts to sleep top and tail with your business partners – right?'

'It was over a year ago now anyway!' The truth never failed to cut deep. We continue to sip on our Mochas, the warm radiating into our cold hands, whilst a brief silence tiptoes around us, broken only by the boisterous entry of a group of teenage French students. I sense Kimberly is building up to some wise words as she sits up, adjusts her bosoms, licks her glossy lips and places her hand upon mine. *Gosh, those hands are incredibly soft.* Her puppy eyes draw me in.

'Look, Rob, I just really care about you and hate to see you wasting your life in the hope that Max will change. And maybe he will. But how much heartache, tears and years are you willing to waste before that may happen?'

She gives my hand a little squeeze that says a message more than a 1000 words could and I try to give a smile of thanks in return. Despite being six years younger than me, she seems emotionally more mature than I could ever be. 'You are better than this, Robbie. Why can't you see that?'

'You are so frigging strong, Kim – are you sure you are not a lesbian, haha?' I was always so derogatory about lesbian women but it was only ever intended to be playful.

'I can safely say I love the penis, thank you, Mr Sparks. Unfortunately for me, the only men I get to hang out with are also my competitors,' chuckles Kimberly as she ruffles my mop of curly hair with her colourful talons. 'When you have had a lifetime of dealing with the male species and their infidelity, you become a wise old owl.' She breaks out into a hysterical laugh with a complimentary snort that makes the French visitors chuckle.

'Kimberly, you are 24, not 54. How many bloody men have there been?'

'Oh that is for another time, Mr Let's just focus on getting you sorted.'

We talk about her latest fashion purchases and her foul taste in men for the next 40 minutes or so before the reality of life persuades us to move on.

Chapter Three

Another day, another interview and yet another rejection. For six months, I have been desperately trying to secure employment. Those three long years in university and the extraordinary costs now seemed so pointless. Every interviewer gives the same feedback:

'You don't have enough experience...'
'The other candidates were stronger...'
'Your grades are not good enough...'

Blah blah blah – it is all just noise now to my already down-trodden spirit. The dream of working for a leading IT power player has long since passed. This is now about being able to be independent, and maintain some sense of self-worth and value. And yet, even the franchised coffee houses fail to provide me with the opportunity to exercise my male pride, forcing me to reluctantly tap into Daddy's money. Max continues to cover our monthly expenses but I do not wish for him to pay for my new interview suit or for his own birthday and Christmas gifts.

Despite the apparent milder winter, the air still maintains its wintery assault. As usual, I struggle to turn the key to the main door of the apartment, leading to irrational irritation on account of my frustrations in the job market.

'Fuck!' I yell out as I kick out and fling my arms to the air.

Thankfully, my neighbour comes to my rescue and pulls the door open as she prepares to enter the nippy air with her infant smothered in blankets like cotton candy. I realise I do not even know her name despite having lived at opposite ends of the corridor for the past two years. My level of self-absorption smirks back at me. I was not always like this, I reflect. But being with Max seems to have zapped my social skills: notably in the last six months since the realisation of the status of our relationship has made herself known. When you question your value in someone's life, you start to question the value of life, full stop. I cease to interact where possible, managing only the occasional smile if really necessary.

Stepping into the lift, my shabby look reflects back. It's not hard to understand the rejection from so many interviews when you share your fashion sense with the homeless man on the corner of Oxford Street. Sound bites of my mother's irritating voice lecturing me about my unruly curls are on playback. The image of my father stares back at me in the lift mirror. My physical resemblance to him is uncanny, though I do not think I have ever seen him looking less than perfect. Image is everything and vanity runs deep. I see the disappointment in his eyes. No doubt, I will endure wasted minutes listening to the successes and highs in the life of Hugh, his high flying nephew, my cousin, when we next meet. I sometimes wonder if Hugh and I were mixed up at the hospital. The toffee-nosed city boy resembles my father more than I could ever desire to. The lift continues to drag itself up the long shaft to the top floor. The cold seems to be taking its toll. All I want to do now is run a hot, deep bath and lie there indefinitely. Max and I have barely spoken for the past eight days. Yes he talks, but I do not listen. I know most of what he says is a lie, a cover up for some other misdemeanour. I wonder if he even notices that I do not talk back. *Maybe he prefers it this way?*

Entering the spacious living space, I kick off my boots like a troublesome teenager and drop to the overly large sofa below, the cushions still scattered around the floor from last night. The wintery view outside is partially covered by the intrusive TV that reflects only my sorry self. Reaching for the remote, something suddenly startles me. Faint muffled sounds whisper from the master bedroom. Quickly realising the day of the week, I remember it cannot be Elsa, the elderly Spanish lady who cleans the apartment twice a week. My heart picks up tempo as the uncertainty of what lies beyond the door grows. It sounds human but there are no words, just similar to the sound one would make if being smothered by an oversized pillow.

I go to the door, lower the polished steel handle and gingerly push it open. A rush of manly air comes dancing out that carries a pungent mixture of unfamiliar cologne, fresh sweat and other bodily fluids. It is unpleasant, yet, in comparison to the visual that is now on display, it is somewhat insignificant. There, on top of the white Egyptian sheets, lay a naked perspiring figure in all his cheating, twisted, fucked-up glory. I cannot comprehend the scene. Despite my analysis of the room, I fail to understand what I am seeing. Max is star-fished and strapped to each corner of the Moroccan antique bed. *I hate that bed.* Leather straps and buckles hold him captive. His masculine chest that is dappled in fine dark hair rises and falls with excitement. But this is no ordinary prisoner. This is some sort of sexual kidnapping and the sight of his throbbing manhood confirms that Max is not being held against *his* will. To the side of Max lay some sort of paddle and a dildo big enough to satisfy two hungry men. The leather semi-mask that partially covers Max's head and eyes provides me with a degree of invisibility. I stand frozen at my point of entry. Is this some sort of strange masturbation ritual that Max engages in when alone? *I always knew he was kinky.*

'I can hear you breathing, baby,' moans Max seductively. Maybe I am not as undetectable as I had thought. 'Come let me fuck you again. I beg you. Ride me harder than the last time…'

What the hell! The gut wrenching blow of reality is too difficult to absorb as an adolescent of barely legal age steps out of the en-suite, yelping with fright at the sight of me brewing a storm of anger that shames any tropical storm. The hairless *boy* stands still like a startled deer facing the headlamps of death. His body – perfection. Golden and perfectly sculptured. *I hate him.* His erection drops quickly and shrivels neatly away as if seeking asylum from the fear that is now all consuming. Max remains unaware but the silent commotion seems to be adding to his excitement.

'Oh yeah, you little tease. Come to Daddy…'

I feel only disgust for Max, yet my anger continues to strangle, preventing me from uttering a single word. And then it comes. The point of no return. The point at which my life would change forever. As anger releases her grip, I launch forward, knocking the lean yet weightless teenager from his feet. The frantic sounds and initial screams alarm Max who remains hostage. I drag the twink from his feet and push him against the wardrobe door, knocking the glass lamp from its stand. The glass shatters, sending shrapnel across the floor in every direction. *He* is panic stricken but I cannot stop. I need to hurt someone. A single blow to the face, though my lack of street fighting skills is reflected in that attempt. It is not *his* face I see but Max's. A second punch. A third, as tears roll down my cheeks, a reflection of the release of hurt. Right at this moment, my heart is broken. I cannot make a fairy tale from this scenario. I cannot ignore the reality of *this* situation and turn a blind eye. The blood of a secret lover is now on my hands. The unknown intruder in my life does not move but whimpers like a wounded hound. Max is in a frenzy but his lover did a good job tying him to the bed so he is going nowhere anytime soon. A series of expletives is the only contribution Max can offer. I do not recognise myself. I have never hurt another person in my life and yet my anger fuels a hatred so evil, it scares me. I see only red. The colour of rage. The colour of hell and now the colour of blood. The sex slave slips slowly down the wardrobe, a combination of shock and pain knocking him out cold. He continues to breath. *Unfortunately.* He is now lying as helpless on the floor as his master on the bed above him: both equally pathetic. A part of me feels shame, but my rage smothers me still.

'What the hell is going on? Fucking untie me right now! Jake? Are you okay?' Max is clearly in a panic and now the limp, fragile body has a name. I am paralysed. Is it fear, guilt or pleasure? I need to think quickly. I am not going to risk facing prosecution for hurting *Jake*. Not because of Max and his consistent need to shag every man in town.

Think, Robbie! For Christ's sake, think God-damnit! Max is unaware of anyone else being in the room. I could just creep out of the apartment, returning hours later pretending to be oblivious to the situation that had taken place at Room 173, Carlton House at 2pm. But how could I face Max and not speak of what I have witnessed? And how can I lie to the police who would surely interview me? What if the boy recognises me as the attacker who had interrupted his sex-a-thon? I know I have to leave. There can be no positive outcome for me regardless of how the next few hours will unfold.

I take one final look at my surroundings, my home. The place where for far too long I naively thought Max and I would grow old or even raise a family. All those hopes and dreams are all now packing up, and leaving right before my eyes, pulling a heavy load on my already shattered heart. The sight of the weasel squirming on the bed, frantically trying to free his pathetic gimp mask is the closing act that signals for my departure. Stepping over the lifeless body below me, I reach inside my bedside drawer, and grab my passport and credit card, and not a single item more.

Still dabbled in the blood of another, I fall against the entrance door of Kimberly's apartment. Within seconds, the door flies open.

'My God, Robbie! What the hell has happened?' Her blouse is unbuttoned slightly and she is sporting bed hair. A lean and overly hairy lad appears in the background minus a t-shirt.

'Babe? Everything okay?' he inquires.

'You… out now! Kimberly shouts without even looking at him.

'What?'

'Time for you to leave. My friend needs me. Out!'

The guy does not argue, and scurries around dressing and gathering his belongings, totally addled. 'Shall I call you…?' he gingerly asks.

'Bye.' With that, I am being pulled into her apartment and the door slams behind us.

'Kim, you didn't need to do that. I didn't know you had a visitor.'

'Did you see how hairy he was,' she giggles. 'You saved me from having to pluck those hairs from between my teeth later on.'

I cannot help but laugh at this but before long, my giggles turn to tears as my pain finally finds an opportunity to escape in the loving arms of one of the few people who has ever truly loved me.

Chapter Four

'But why bloody Indonesia?' screeches Kimberly. 'Where is it anyway?'

Stood in departures, it is the first time I have smiled since my mortifying discovery 48 hours previous. As always, my trusted friend was there to pick up the pieces, providing a bed, food and a good talking to. She refused to allow me to return to my apartment, giving Max any opportunity to talk me around and instead, took me shopping for some tropical weather essentials, courtesy of my credit card that Max will receive the bill for. The swift change of SIM card provided a sense of anonymity from Max. *I wonder if he has even noticed you have gone?*

My head is spinning as I contemplate my impending travel. What will I do for work? How will I manage financially? *Daddy's got this one covered, kid!* Where will I live? I notice a single Disney tear doing a slow waltz down Kimberley's cheek. She is dressed like a grieving widow today – forever the drama queen. Her black ensemble is modest by her standards though entry into any House of God would still not be permitted. I chuckle as I notice her black pump shoes.

'Ms Jones! Why on earth are you in a pair of less than sexy flats?' I ask.

'I am in no state of mind to be concerned with my appearance when I am losing my best friend to some oriental country.'

I try not to laugh at Kimberly who is clearly upset but the fact that she has still attached her two layers of false lashes and blow dried her hair to a height of at least 10cm indicates her vanity is not completely crushed.

'Hey Hun. Indonesia is not oriental. It is near Thailand and Malaysia. *She still looks confused.* Okay it is near Australia.'

'Oh my God! That's worse. That's the other side of the frigging world.' Kimberley is now wailing, bringing unwanted attention to us.

'Kimberly… Hun… I need to do this. If I am to move on from Max, I need the physical space between us. Remember how many times we have talked about my adventures in Indonesia? Ever since I first visited there in my gap year, I have felt a sense of peace whenever I am there. Before I met Max, I would return each summer. I had even hoped that maybe Max and I would visit there…' Emotion clogs my throat as I reflect back on the good times with Max. I see his handsome face smiling back at me but then my anger reignites and I see only Jake straddled on top of him, and I am recomposed.

'But you don't know anyone there. I am not there.' More tears, more drama.

I place my hands either side of her face and tilt her face gently towards me.

'Listen. You remember Ali from University, right?'

'Crazy Asian with the very cute face I recall.'

'I am not sure that is terribly PC, Kim.'

'I always felt he had a little thing for you, Robbie.'

'Really?' Kimberly's comments distract me slightly. 'Yes him. Well, he is back in Indonesia, and has offered me a place to stay and thinks he can line up some freelance web design work with a company he represents. I have to do this, Kimberly. You can visit.' I give her the biggest reassuring smile that I can muster. Puppy eyes on turned on to maximum effect, she grins back,

'Why didn't you tell me this earlier? I would have slept better last night knowing there is someone waiting there for you,' Kimberly states, appearing slightly bemused

'Sorry, Kim, things were just so chaotic. I was not thinking straight and I only confirmed things with Ali last minute,' I try to explain though she seems distracted and not really listening to my explanation.

'Do they have shopping malls in Indonesia?' We both burst out laughing as she pulls me in for the tightest hug possible – squashed right in between her mammaries as the final call for departure indicates my need to leave. I take a final look at the amazing woman standing, crying in front of me, knowing that I have no intention of ever returning.

*****

The 16-hour flight feels longer than I remember and the final hour has dragged. Too much time to think. To reflect. Inevitably, thoughts keep returning to Max. Four years is a long time invested. One moment you are with someone day in, day out and the next, they are gone. There are post-traumatic emotions that need to be worked through and so far, I have experienced a different one each hour – hatred, anger, longing, love, confusion. I imagined Max tracking me down at Kimberly's and begging for my forgiveness. It hurts that he did not come kicking the door down and dragging me back home like a Neanderthal. I am not sure he would have gotten past Kimberly though. But he could have tried… right? Deep down, I knew I prolonged my departure at the airport in the delusional hope that Max would come pounding up, pushing through the crowds until finally reaching me and publicly sharing a declaration of love. Did he just not care? Was he equally as unhappy as I was and is glad that I have finally left? Maybe he considered me a drain on his resources? Or maybe I was not sexually exciting enough for him anymore. Whatever his reasons, it hurts. My mind will not settle. I wonder if Max is even bothered that I have left? Will he have called the police when I failed to return home or did he simply just load up *Grindr* and do what he does best? And my parents? How long will it take for them to notice the email I sent informing them of my departure? For sure, they will not have shared this information with Max considering how much they detest the guy. I know my parents are not exactly homophobic but Max seems to rouse in them something similar. After all, they had not disowned me when I told them of my sexuality on my 18th birthday since all hell had broken out in our household that night. I don't know if I will ever forget the sound of my mother weeping because my father had been "entertaining" a client instead of taking his family to dinner on such an important occasion. When I finally plucked up the courage to say the

22

words, 'I'm gay!' my mother asked if I would like a cup of tea and my father asked me to pass the remote control. It was probably an inconvenience for me to bring up such a thing during one of their battles.

My mother had looked unamused by my revelation. All pearls and tweed, I struggle to remember the last kind word she has offered or gentle maternal touch she gave. She wasn't always like this. Jean Sparks had once been a fiery young Scottish lass who aspired to be something so much more. She took to the role of dutiful wife to Charlie at the expense of her own aspirations, though the luxury lifestyle afforded to her by her husband's success somewhat softens the sacrifices in love and life she has made. But years of catching your husband in the arms of another, often younger, woman has taken its toll. I think she resents my father, yet, after 35 years of marriage, lacks the confidence to go at it alone. So she does as many women in her situation do. She turns a blind eye to the extra-curricular activities of her husband and settles for her healthy monthly allowance in exchange. The ladies at the Wimbledon Country Club provide her with companionship and I have always been convinced that her tennis coach, Mike, is a little more hands on than his role requires.

And what of Charlie Sparks, the original gigolo. My father is everything I am not and everything I would never want to be. He is obsessed with money, incredibly materialistic and has this uncanny ability to make everyone around him feel like a purchase. He solves problems with money, shows affection in cash and tries to buy his way out of the multiple compromising positions he has found himself in over the years. He confidence is sky high and still rising. The only thing I am thankful to him for, is his physical attributes. A strikingly handsome man with a full head of dark curls that are slightly peppered on the sides; he attracts the eye of many a lady. His olive skin and slightly hairy body reflects his Mediterranean ancestry which I am grateful to have received. Sadly, his height was not bestowed to me and my smaller 5'9 frame has frequently stood intimidated by him. I think he loathes Max because he sees him as a competitor in terms of success or bank balance, rather than because of what physical acts he does with his son. My father is very self-obsessed and therefore, everything becomes about him. The fact that Max has made more money than my father by the age of just 39 from the stock market probably really irritates my competitive Dad.

The first and only meeting between my parents and Max had been strained to say the least. I suspect my father had an impending "appointment" to shag and our meeting was going to hold him up. When Max tried to break the icy air that blew amongst the silence by stating how much he loved me, my mother responded with, 'Yes, thank you, Max, we don't need to talk about that now. I will make a cup of tea for everyone'. The temperature once again plummeted. One thing I am certain of is that my father would have been more than delighted when I refused to accept his financial assistance in my final two years at Uni and instead agreed to allow Max to pay. Max vowed never to sit through such an awkward moment again and as my parents have never requested so much as a coffee together, I guess they feel the same way.

As the plane lands abruptly, I am shaken out of my vacation to memory lane. I feel numb and exhausted, yet the excitement of the adventure ahead tries to take control. I am proud that I refuse to follow my mother's destiny. Proud that I have not settled for comfortable. Proud that I am not driven by the same material dreams of my father. Here I stand. On the tarmac of Denpasar Airport, Bali – shit scared but never bloody happier.

Chapter Five

The Balinese immigration officers remain as cute as I remember during the onset of my love with this country back ten years ago. It had been my father's way of dealing with my sexual revelation. Rather than a hug and some kind words of reassurance, he offered a year long trip around Asia. Maybe he thought I would "find myself" like that neurotic character from *Eat, Pray, Love,* or better still that I would return "straight". Whatever his motive, it was no real surprise as this was how he dealt with "difficult" situations. My mother was playing more tennis than ever, *much to the pleasure of Mike, no doubt,* so had paid little attention to my trip back then. It had meant delaying my enrolment at University, much to the unhappiness of Kimberly as we had planned to study at the same college. I briefly wonder how she is feeling now that I have abandoned her for a second time in favour of lying low on the Indonesian Archipelago.

My excitement of re-acquainting with Ali distracts me somewhat from my sombre thoughts. I always had a bit of a secret crush on Ali. When we first met in the course registration queue during Fresher's Week, there was something so attractive about him. Of course, I was already deeply in love with Max. *My god, Max. I miss him so much.* Ali was a living memory of my brief affair with Indonesia before my life with Max. He reminded me of why I loved the people so much: impeccably well-mannered and incredibly humble. The thing I remember most about Ali is his compulsive need to smile. He was in awe of being in London and it was expressed permanently. Initially, I had no idea he was gay; I have not exactly been skilled at detecting others from my community. I just found him rather adorable and without question, handsome. I also enjoyed that his shorter 5'5 frame actually made me feel tall.

My happy memories suppress my ongoing heartache. I refuse to allow her ugly face to show, as the cutest of the Indonesian officers requests for me to step forward to the overly large wooden counter.

'Hey, American – step forward.' The enthusiastic family behind me give a gentle nudge forward.

'I'm... I'm British actually.'

'Selamat Datang – welcome to Indonesia. Passport please.'

The wait is incredibly long and the suffocating heat compresses me from all sides. A stark contrast to the UK chill I have left behind. Time was surely moving slower under the Balinese heat. If ever there was a passenger to suspect of smuggling drugs into the country then my paranoid behaviour of constantly looking over my shoulder and shuffling my feet, was making me the perfect profile. No matter how hard I try to fit in with the other sweaty tourists, I can't help but still look suspicious. Despite being a hardened traveller, I have never mastered the art of not looking like an actual tourist. I frequently stand confused in a street holding a map upside down, puzzled expression on my face and with no sense of direction, I often have to resort to catching overly expensive cabs in order to get back to my hotels that I have no possibility of locating.

'Sir. There. Is. A. Problem.' Each word is spoken in isolation to perfection. Is this where I am wrongfully arrested for smuggling. *Smuggling what? Sun cream?* Ali had made no secret of the level of corruption and injustice in his country, and with his father being a police officer, he was surely well informed.

'Sir. Need visa on arrival first. Please join that queue,' signals the officer. 'Terimah Kasih.'

The feeling of relief at not having to deal with a more serious matter after a long-haul flight is welcomed, though there is a flicker of disappointment I won't receive a full body search from the officer. The view in the distance is just as I remember. The lush green foliage forms a beautiful front to the sapphire backdrop.

Sixty minutes or so later, and I am finally through immigration, *sadly, without my handsome officer* and into the Island of Gods. A crowd of locals stand waiting for loved ones, wearing traditional Balinese clothing. The beauty of the people here never fails to impress me. The women are incredibly sophisticated and impeccably turned out. They demonstrate that beauty and modesty can have a symbiotic relationship. Something Kimberly could learn a thing or two about. The colourful hijabs of the smaller number of Muslim women forms a beautiful rainbow across the sea of people waiting. No sign of Mr Sudario but I am not concerned. Ali was never on time for a single lecture in our three years together at Uni and it is this laid-back attitude that I admire in him, almost aspire to be like. In many other ways, Ali has become very westernised, probably the result of being able to live his life as he wanted away from the religious and cultural constraints of his family during the four years he spent in the UK. Ali is Muslim, which is less common on this island where about 85% of the 4 million population adhere to Balinese Hinduism. I believe, it was the constraints of his religion, coupled with the traditions of his Balinese culture that led Ali to go a little wild in London. I can recall our first night out in one of the gay hotspots of Central London and seeing Ali's eyes light up like a fat child in a candy store. He was overwhelmed and most definitely over-excited. I think I counted four or five snogs he enjoyed with various men that night. The intolerance to alcohol, a new substance for Ali, partly attributed to that behaviour. That same night, Ali had kissed me, well, attempted to. It didn't mean anything, well, not at the time. *Maybe Kimberly was right? She is terribly perceptive after all.* I had put it down to Ali's drunken state. I am not sure he even remembered it. But I do know that my fondness for Ali ignited on that night. I guess a part of me was a little jealous seeing him exploring his new self with other strangers and I wanted to be the one to educate him. From such emotions grew a wonderfully strong friendship for which I am grateful and the healthy level of flirting we have enjoyed ever since, never hurt anyone.

I send a quick text message to Kimberly to reassure her that I have landed safely. Returning my phone to my pocket, I take a slow meander around the arrivals hall, soaking in the ambience of this Asian jewel and enjoy my re-acquaintance with the mouth-watering cuisine. The blend of spices explodes in my mouth as I close my eyes to savour the flavours. 'Mr Sparks. Welcome back to the most beautiful place on Earth where all the beautiful people are created,' Ali breaks out into a hysterical giggle.

'How did you find me?' I ask, desperately trying to clear my mouth of satay.

'I saw your white skin glowing in the distance,' he chuckles. His accent never fails to make me smile. Ali's English is impeccable but he has never lost the Indonesian accent and sometimes the pronunciation of some words makes me affectionately smile. His slight frame is a little more muscular than I remember and the piercing heat has coated Ali a few shades darker than when in London just six months ago.

'I told you that man was no good, Robbie. You need a sexy Asian to show you how a real man loves,' laughs Ali as he throws his arms around me, highlighting the difference in our height.

'Someone like you, Ali?' I tease

'Nah, I tell you many times, Mr You are not my type. That white skin makes you look half-dead. We need to get you to Kuta beach for some sun and surf. People here have never seen something so pale.' Ali gives me one of his incredible smiles that enables me to feel safe for the first time in a long time.

As we exit the crowded airport terminal, we are confronted with packs of hunters touting for business. 'Taxi, Taxi.'

'Where you going? Cheap taxi.'

'G'day, bro?' asks one of the younger guys, clearly mistaking me for one of the more familiar Aussie tourists who come to Bali in the same numbers that the Brits arrive in Spain each year. I am so grateful that Ali can steer me through the crowds, though when we arrive at our transport, I consider retreating. 'What the hell, Ali? Where's the limo? Actually, where's the car, never mind the frigging limo?' I cannot help but laugh at the sight of my airport transfer – a moped. 'Well, it's a good job I travelled light then,' I joke, as I hop on to the back and strap on my backpack and grab Ali for dear life.

'Hold on, Mr,' he shouts back to me as we race out of the airport compound and out into Denpasar – the main gateway into Bali. Wind in my somewhat thinning hair, the midday sun surfing across my face and I feel truly incredible. I never did understand why I left this Eden in the first place. This is the start of something amazing I confirm with myself. A second chance to grab my fair share of happiness. Distant echoes of doubt can be heard in my mind but I exchange them for positive possibilities only.

The City of Denpasar is the most populous province of Bali and one of the top Asian tourist destinations. It may not be the tropical paradise of Ubud or Nusa Dua but its mystical allure is still just as appealing. Accelerating past the Catur Muka statue, I receive my first of many welcomes from the local people. A group of young children stand at a crossing and wave excitedly as if welcoming some dignitaries. The Balinese people are so inquisitive. They enjoy meeting others and like to know more about the visitors that they are hosting. The black and white gingham sarongs draping the menacing doorway protectors of the various temples gives me that comforting sense of familiarity. Sun drenched backpackers sip on Bintangs as they dodge the countless daily offerings to the Great Gods and Goddesses that paper the pathways.

The fifteen-minute journey brings us to the colourful sub district of Kuta. Originally home to hard-core backpackers back in the 1980s, this village has worked hard to improve its infrastructure in an attempt to attract a wider mix of tourists. I never fail to be amazed by the tiny alleyways that the countless mopeds negotiate in and out of, and the poorly planned buildings that sit confused around them. I cannot pretend that Kuta is my favourite Balinese spot but the chaos, I find charming and knowing Ali as well as I do, I know this is all about partying my woes away for the next three nights before we get to move on to Ali's place in a more tranquil part of the island.

Chapter Six

With no time to unpack and unwind, and despite my pleas for mercy on account of my jet-lag, Ali takes us on a 10 minute, high-speed bike ride arriving in Seminyak. Destination – Dhyana Pura. Best known for its relatively new strip of gay bars and clubs, the location provides the perfect hunting ground for *bule* or "white-man" hunters. Ali senses my discomfort and pulls me in closer as if to ward off my potential predators. The music is loud yet the atmosphere struggles to be electric. Four or five bars sit side by side with little noticeable differences between each one. The same style of music screams out of the open doorways and ribbons of men stream out onto the streets outside. The clientele are generally small and exotic with sun-kissed skin, and the blackest of hair. The leanness of Balinese men has always captivated me, though never in a desiring way. A handful of impressive drag queens take to the stage as Ali's friends, Cahyo and Denny, greet us at the entrance, and lead the way into bar number one.

I am not the biggest fan of men in drag, and try to disguise my uncomfortable persona, though as the Japanese spectator is dragged onto the stage and stripped to his unflattering underwear, I feel particularly challenged. I can't deny their talent to entertain. The lip singing rivals any of Britney's performances and the legs on some of the "stars" would be the envy of many a girl. After a rather impressive rendition of *Born this Way,* the over-bright lighting returns, where I find myself being stalked by an attractive, pale-skinned guy whom I assume is of mixed-race due to his unusually tall stature. His eyes are fixated on me, never failing to look away, though we occasionally lose sight of each other as the passing crowds stumble out onto the streets. Ali is in full swing entertainment mode in my left ear but I am not listening to a word. I am like a deer. Stalked. Frozen. Fixated on the hunter in front of me. I love the chase. Always have. I take a coy sip of my flamboyant cocktail before returning to the stare-off only to find my suitor in the arms of another and much older westerner.

'His loss!' shouts Ali's friend Cahyo from the opposite side of the table.

'I don't know what you mean,' I respond, slightly embarrassed that someone has witnessed my failed attempt at flirting.

'You are just a bit out of touch, Mr. That dick in London drained you of all your smouldering hotness. We'll get it back,' jokes Ali.

I know it is too soon to be looking for someone. My heart still sits in the hands of *that* rat. I refocus, and enjoy the night with Ali and my new Balinese friends, thinking I will certainly learn some techniques from these three amigos.

A stream of cocktails, a concoction of shots and the whole scene looks completely different. My barriers are down and my thirst for fun is at an all-time high. Taking a much needed pee stop in bar number two, I negotiate the masses of man meat before me. My perked pecs take a number of "hits" as the over-confident men take a cheeky feel. It is not until the third grope that I look up and catch the eye of a rather dishy muscular Asian. His full lips hijack my attention, and as he seductively bites on the lower one and whips his tongue across the top, I wonder if someone has pressed slow-mo. With alcohol raving through my veins, I have the confidence to lean forward and sample the taste of his kiss. The effect is instant. My groin swells and my heart rate races. Stranger man yanks me in closer and I can feel the swelling in his shorts pressing against my thigh. Awareness of my surroundings is AWOL, and all I can focus on is the way his tongue circles my mouth and teases my own tongue. The need to pee is now stronger than ever so I reluctantly pull myself away, giving a seductive wink as I turn to move towards the toilet. Of course, in reality, I know my wink is probably anything but seductive and I most likely have dribble running down my chin. But for now, I feel hot and in control, and so I am going to run with it. The relief from peeing is immense and as I start to button up my jeans, I feel the presence of another behind me. The light is dim but I recognise the smell. It is my mysterious Asian. His hands firmly grope my arse before his left arm swoops across my chest and up under my neck as if almost in a head lock. He bites my left ear lobe and I shiver with excitement. His plump lips attach to the right side of my neck and he bites me with a sexy, yet slightly aggressive force. My knees tremble as his hand spreads open under my neck forcing my head to lean backwards into his shoulder. He whispers into my right ear but I hear no words only sounds, the hot slow breaths raising my temperature. I force myself from his hold and turn my body to face him. Eye to eye, I realise the extent of his beauty and the fact that he is here with me in this moment restores a little of my confidence.

'Come home with me,' he whispers.

'I don't even know your name.'

'Raden. *Now* will you come home with me?'

I am tempted. More than tempted – I am unquestionably convinced. The doors flies open and in falls Ali. 'Hey. This is a girls' night. No boys allowed. Get your arse back out there and start drinking. Mr Handsome – you will have to wait until another day.'

Ali is in hysterics as he drags me away from *my* Raden, giving me only enough time to look back and bite my bottom lip and whisper, 'Sorry.' I love Ali for this. He knows what is best for me more than I know myself and I need to heal a little before I start playing around. But I take a moment to pat myself on the back – the hunted has just become the hunter and it feels *so* bloody great to be back.

Chapter Seven

Another night and another bar. Having convinced Ali that we needed to go somewhere more up market, we were now suited and mingling (or mincing would be a more accurate description) around the luxurious three floors of the exclusive club, *The Cage*. Despite Ali not being officially "out", he is incredibly well connected in the LGBTI community as he is involved in a lot of web design work for many prominent organisations; hence, our projection to the front of the queue. The club is located on the outskirts of the city and is less obviously catering for men who like men. There are no rainbow flags flying high. No drag queens parading the perimeters and the patriots are mixed – but I figured this was to guise the club from unwanted attention. Generally, the Balinese are very accepting of all people, but as in many South East Asian countries, homosexuality is something that is just not acknowledged. They know it exists, and they know that there are bars and clubs of this nature, but the people would rather not talk about it.

The club is set back a little from the bustle of the main road and the tree lined street provides yet another form of camouflage. The building is modern and bold with clear lines, and expanses of tinted glass windows. It reminds me of a number of stacking boxes arranged unevenly. Ali informs me that most of the men are professionals with a lot of money to spend so it should be a cheap night for us if we flirt well. Many of the men are either still rummaging around in the back of the closet or living a double life – married by day and prowling for men by night. Ali loves the "straight" guys as their lack of commitment suits his needs well. After all, his family has a plan for him to marry next year so the last thing he needs is a needy, dependent boyfriend to manage.

'I'll get a drink to get us started,' I shout across at Ali, competing with the deafening base of the music.

The bar is very plush with a soft glow highlighting the name of the establishment in the centre. Row after row of champagne glasses sit like soldiers, clearly setting the tone. No shots and happy hours here, I think to myself. The bartenders are clearly employed on the basis of their looks – sculpted faces, perfect skin and muscular bodies. It is easy to just stand here in complete adoration and watch them – though slightly perverted, I figure. I take a quick sly photo and send it to Kimberly with the tag, *Wish you were here!* I am one of a few white men in the club and judging by the lack of attention, I figure this is not going to be my hunting ground tonight. Scanning the room, I notice Ali whispering into the ear of a slightly older guy. His face is familiar and as he turns completely to my direction, I recall the photo that Ali had sent me when he first met this guy about six months ago. Ali's sugar daddy, as I like to call him, is a top plastic surgeon in Kuala Lumpur. Married with two children, he frequently flies to Bali for some "release". He and Ali are not in any exclusive form of a relationship, but judging by the body language, Ali is not too pleased to see him here tonight without having known about it. My phone bleeps and right on cue, Kimberly has responded.

You are such a slut, Mr Sparks – but I love it! Miss you so much. Come back now! xxx. I cannot help but smile at her messages. They ooze her personality. Happy thoughts of my close friend preoccupy me and I fail to notice I now have company.

'Sir, Mr Permana at the VIP seating area has asked me to give you two glasses of Moët.' The voice is coming from a rather tall, well-dressed man who seems to be working for someone rather than out enjoying a drink. He is wearing the classic black suit bodyguard ensemble with the standard Bluetooth earpiece in his right ear.

'Thank you. But who exactly is Mr Permana?' I ask, sounding slightly ungrateful.

'Sir, enjoy the drinks.' And off he walks, the mystery of my suitor intriguing me all the more. Ali continues to question his lover so I gulp back the first champagne and then decide it would be more appropriate to sip on the second. I casually scan the room trying to look indifferent as I crave to know the identity of my admirer. The view from the bar is limited so I take my drink and meander around. I notice a number of elegantly dressed women dotted around and wonder if they are high-end fag hags or lesbians. I do not linger on this thought for too long, too consumed by intrigue for Mr P. The VIP seating area is not clearly visible from the main club area so I reluctantly retrace my steps back to the bar, admiring the gothic decor of the club on route. The contrast between the inside and outside space clashes, yet it works.

'Did you enjoy your drink, or should I say, drinks?'

I don't even notice the guy talking as I brush past him, turning only briefly to acknowledge his question.

'Yes, thank you.'

'I had intended for one to be for your friend,' he laughs. 'But if you are thirsty, I can get you another.'

My cheeks start to flush as I now realise I am in the presence of Mr Permana – whomever he may be. Slowly, I lift my head, trying desperately to contain my teenage grin. I am not prepared for what stands before me. Mr P is dashing. He is the man from the cover of Men's Health, the heart throb from TV, the epitome of hotness. His hand is outstretched to greet me as I stand gawping. His left eyebrow raises slightly, and his plump lips subtly pout and grin all at once.

'Mr Permana?' I ask, all blushful.

'Um, you can call me Rifqi. Selamat Malam or Good Evening as you say.' The accent melts chocolate and the mouth from which the words dance is perfection. Two rows of perfectly white teeth stand like centurions, surrounded by two dark, pink pillows. The smile is wide and reflects in the eyes that are hypnotising me as he continues to talk.

'Would you care to join me for a drink?'

Knowing that Ali is probably engaged in an all-night domestic, I graciously accept Rifqi's offer as I am led to a small booth in the corner of the VIP lounge. I sense that many eyes are glaring but Rifqi reassures me and places his hand on my shoulder. I notice his muscular torso as his fitted white shirt snugs him closer. The opening at the neckline reveals a caramel coloured, smooth complexion. A large bottle of Moët is brought to the table without request and I start to consider the importance of the man I am sat opposite. *Why are so many people fussing around him?*

'Are all these people your staff?' I casually ask. Rifqi laughs out loud shaking his head.

'God, no. The guy you met earlier – Wahyu, is with me. He is my personal assistant. Though he insists on trying to look like one of my… um, how do you say in English… heavies?'

'And what is it that you do for work exactly?'

'Oh, nothing important,' smiles Rifqi as he signals with his hand as if dismissing Wahyu.

Despite not being a native English speaker, his vocabulary is incredible and the conversation flows so easily, yet he has retained his Indonesian accent which makes him even more adorable.

Chapter Eight

'Someone got lucky last night,' sniggers Ali.

'It was not like that,' I grin. This is actually an honest response. There were no seedy tales to tell. No girly gossip to share about an all-night session with my handsome lover. No, last night was something so unique. Something I have never experienced before. Romance. Romance in the Hollywood movie sense of the word. The kind of romance I have craved but had started to give up on. I was not really prepared to share my story with Ali on this occasion. I figured that by keeping it to myself, the memory would last longer.

With Ali busy in the kitchen, I tease myself with a montage of images, sound-bites and memories from the previous 10 hours.

Rifqi had hypnotised me with his stories and tales of his life growing up in his hometown of Jogyakarta as we sipped on our expensive bubbles, yet he skilfully avoided revealing too much detail. It was all quite superficial but captivated me all the same. I think he could have just been mumbling a string of random words and I would have still been attentive. It was the tones and intonation in his voice. Bali was his second home. A place where he felt comfortable in his own skin, away from the prying eyes of his Muslim family. He was so easy to talk to. His energy was so calming. I felt so attracted to him, yet it was not purely physical lust. *Yes but that body was something else, right?* His passing touches were brief yet electrifying as he gently placed a reassuring hand on my shoulder or brushed my blushing cheeks with his slender fingers. My intrigue for this man was on another level. I was in the palm of his hand listening to his every word as if listening to some wise prophet. His ability to make me feel special was a gift. The questioning

– subtle, as he attempted to find out a little more about me with each passing hour, though never pressing for the information he intuitively knew I was omitting. I did not want to reveal too much too soon and run the risk of him retreating.

The flirting was evident but had class. A means in itself rather than a means of getting me into his bed. Rifqi knew how to compliment, and at the right time and for the sole purpose of making the other person feel special. His words were carefully selected to have impact and were never crass or seedy. There was no spoken indication of wanting to have sex but the body language sang a tune of attraction towards me. He was simmering the chemistry for a later date. For the right time. The only annoyance was the presence of his assistant Wahyu, and a couple of other suited and booted gentleman. They maintained an appropriate distance from us but I was still conscious and a little weary of their presence.

The parting sensual sniff in the cove of my neck sent a pulsating wave of excitement around my bloodstream that weakened my knees.

'Until we meet on Saturday, Mr Sparks. Rest well.' And he was gone.

Eight hours of the most captivating talk had finally drawn to a close as he had his driver drop me off. I had no idea where we were heading on our Saturday date, but I knew it could not come quick enough.

'Noodles or rice?' comes a voice from the kitchen shaking me out of daydream.

'Do you have cornflakes?'

'You are in Asia now, dear. Time to eat like a local.' Ali's infectious giggles echo around the apartment.

'Where's Cahyo and Denny by the way, Ali? I didn't get a chance to thank them for allowing me to stay here. Are they a couple by the way?'

Ali comes skipping into the living space with a massive grin as if he knows a naughty secret but can't resist in sharing it.

'What do you think?' he playfully jests. 'And can you guess who the bottom is?' Ali's giggles turn into an all-out burst of laughter. I was not sure what he found so humorous.

Understandably, it would be a challenge to deduce the sexual roles between Denny and Cahyo as both are rather effeminate.

'Ali, you are a bitch sometimes.' And with that, Ali jumps over the back of the sofa landing right in my lap and plants an overly wet kiss on my lips before skipping off, shrieking of laughter again. I cannot help but smile.

Wandering into the kitchen, the rich aromas of my breakfast feast greet me. It is not my usual spread but my host is eager to supervise my re-acquaintance with the food he is so proud of. Ali was always keen at University to introduce new friends to Indonesian cuisine though I am not sure he ever won Kimberly over. She has always been more of a pie and chips kinda girl. We frequently spent many a night eating to the point of passing out and sharing stories of travel, family life, and if we were really drunk, politics and religion.

'So, Ali, what happened with you and your gentleman friend last night? Things looked a little tense before I went off with Rifqi.'

'He is a spineless shit. He's gotta go. I need to find myself a nice, new, shiny plaything,' he chuckles. I sense he is not as blasé as the role he plays. That's the thing with Ali. He is forever "in role" making it difficult to know when things truly bother him, and hides constantly behind that smile and those giggles. Yet, I see the upset and disappointment in his eyes. Just as I think Ali is about to open up, he retracts and returns to relying upon the humour that's seems to carry him through most challenges.

'I'm choosing to be straight from now on. No more willy for me. Now eat up, my good friend, and start talking about lover man!'

Chapter Nine

Saturday morning has finally arrived after four long days of counting down the hours to my date with Rifqi, only disrupted by our move to Ali's place just outside Downtown Bali. Ali's one bed apartment is going to be a tight squeeze but I am grateful my good friend is kind enough to welcome me into his home until I can set myself up with a job and deposit for my own place.

I expected Rifqi to arrive in a chauffeur driven black Mercedes, so I am a little (though pleasantly) surprised as he revs up on a rather understated moped. *Such a contrast from the image portrayed the other night.* I admit, the thought of spending the day clenching my thighs around his muscular frame and having an excuse to hug him somewhat pleases me.

'Do I get to find out where we are going?' I ask like an excited school girl.

'Just hold on tight. Real tight,' Rifqi sniggers.

His scent is so fresh as I climb on behind him and catch the breeze of coconut oil in his black waves. The excitement of travelling to an unknown place thrills me as we cautiously pull out into the busy weekend traffic. An overwhelming sense of familiarity greets me. Rifqi and I feel so close, so connected, and yet, I tell myself he is still a stranger. A stranger whom I know very little about it. I have not really questioned myself on just how little I do know of this man. Sure, he told me about his successful export business and his life growing up in another city, but there is still so much left to explore. *Slow down, Robbie. Why rush things as usual? Let the Balinese ambience consume you.* My usual lack of geographical awareness prevents me knowing where we are travelling but as Rifqi slows down and steers off the main road, something familiar strikes me

'I know this place!' I shout elated.

'Yeah it's your favourite, I know.'

'So you *were* listening to me last night,' I giggle.

The village of Ubud has always held my heart in her hands. The tranquillity and sense of peace is indescribable. My appreciation of awe and wonder was fully developed during my past encounter, and it is, once again, fully engaged at our reunion. Her beauty, shrouded in mystique, never fails to rouse me. I leap from the moped and rush to the edge of the road, quickly followed by Rifqi who stands proud. Standing at the edge of the roadside, we gaze across the Tegallalang Rice Terraces. The morning mist rolls across the hues of green, creating a mise en scène masterpiece. She sings to me, giving praise to the Hindu Gods that have created and sculptured her artistry. The lush emerald layers seem endless whilst coconut palms reaching for the sky nestle randomly. A lone farmer is visible in the distance. His morning work coming to a close as countless tourists gawk and stare. Two identical gathering baskets balance on either end of the bamboo pole that sits like his crucifix across his shoulders that are no doubt blackened by the intense eastern rays.

Rifqi places a hand on my shoulder and gives a little squeeze that completes the mood. 'Truly magical, isn't it,' he whispers, as if not to stir her from her sleep.

'Selfie time,' I laugh as I pull out my iPhone to capture the moment.

'No!' yells Rifqi moving swiftly out of the field of the camera's vision. The mood changes quickly and the sudden fear that is now oozing from Rifqi scares me. The reaction seems dramatic although unquestionably genuine.

'I'm sorry,' he mournfully pleas. 'I... I... um... I don't do photos.' His attempt to laugh fails to lift the awkwardness pressing down on us. I am puzzled by his reaction. Rifqi is incredible looking and no doubt extremely photogenic so why is he so unwilling to capture this moment together? I sense his embarrassment and feel it best to let things lie unspoken of, yet my mind is racing with questions longing to be heard.

Despite the tension nestling nicely in between us, I suggest we head further into the village and we jump back on the moped. We travel into the centre of the village, pulling up outside the Sacred Monkey Forest Sanctuary: a fun blend of Hindu temples and entertainment, courtesy of the mischievous, long-tailed macaque squatters residing there. We are greeted by a troop of monkeys who sit huddled together on the entrance pillars. The varying size and greying hair of the larger apes suggests they are possibly a family. The grandmother is busily de-fleaing her young grandchild whose siblings are charming a small crowd with their acrobatics. Rifqi stands there smiling which slightly reassures my insecure self. I want to reach out and place my palm inside his but know that this would not be appropriate.

We casually stroll around the peaceful gardens, only occasionally disturbed by the antics of our distant ancestors. The dense foliage and low growing flora protect us from the intense sunlight. The shadowy walkways are eerie and silent. I struggle for conversation, although, I yearn to hear Rifqi's voice. I am overthinking as usual and consider if the photo episode has caused irreparable damage as distance appears to grow between us. *Why do you continue to analyse and pull every single detail apart?*

We climb the steps to a higher point on which sits a small Hindu shrine. I slip on the damp moss but Rifqi grabs my arm, saving me from a dramatic tumble. He pulls me in closer as my giggles consume me, takes a quick panoramic glance around him before planting his soft lips on my forehead. We linger there. Probably for only a few seconds but it feels like minutes. His energy radiates into the deep folds of my busy mind that now instantly slows down and enters a state of serenity. This is where I wish to stand forever. Right in this moment. Right here with *my* Mr Permana. The sound of sandals flip flopping towards us deny us of more time. The unsubtle stares of the hijab cladded older lady clearly indicate her distaste of man on man action. Rifqi looks visibly uncomfortable so I reach out to reassure him. His shoulders tense and his back arches like a startled alley cat. His warm hue now extinguished, Rifqi walks off, picking up the pace as he descends the slippery steps two at time, not once looking back to check on me. So I stop. I stand still and breathe in the pure air circulating in a gentle breeze around me. And I realise, Rifqi is struggling with his sexuality. How could I have not seen this before? After all, I met him at a "discreet" gay bar. It makes sense now. The small tantrum with the photo, the frozen persona when caught canoodling. I sometimes forget the difficulty some people face in accepting their sexuality, or at least, being able to express this, as my own "coming out" went unnoticed. I head back to the sanctuary entrance and feel quite smug like a rookie detective who has solved his first crime.

Rifqi is sat on the step, head in palms. Moving towards him, he notices me, lifts his head up and runs both hands through his thick black hair. He looks visibly stressed.

'I get it now. I understand,' I say smugly.

'I don't think you possibly could,' Rifqi's voice breaks on the last syllable and all I want to do is hug him but that of course is what led to this.

'I know accepting who we are can be difficult, Rifqi. It's okay.'

Rifqi's head snaps quickly towards me and I see anger in his eyes. My heart stops. He controls his emotions and takes a deep breath with his eyes closed before continuing.

'It is not about accepting myself. I know what I am already. But acceptance from others is not even an option. Yet, how could a westerner with all your LGBTI rights possibly understand that. I accept myself. The problem is my family. My people and my religion do not.' Rifqi's eyes drown in tears and he lowers his head, releasing one or two drops to the floor below. I feel helpless. I sit down alongside him, though maintaining an acceptable distance to prevent the gossip of others.

'Do you know what my religion says about people like you and I, Robbie?' He does not wait for my answer. 'They say we will burn in...' The sentence is left incomplete, no doubt not wishing to upset me.

'It's such religious claptrap. How dare other people tell us who we can and cannot love? I know God made me and he does not make mistakes so he must love me all the same.' My reference to God surprises me as I have never considered myself religious to any degree.

43

'Robbie. You need to appreciate that for me, life and religion are symbiotic. One does not exist without the other. It has been ingrained in me by my family from a very young age. My family is incredibly devout and of course, it is complicated because we are...' Rifqi draws a deep breath and sighs but fails to complete yet another sentence. *Why all the mystery?* He turns his face away and stares into the distance.

I cannot empathise with his struggles despite a longing to. I have no religion, a family who seem indifferent and I come from a country that, on the whole, accepts gay people. These emotions that attack Rifqi seem so outdated to me but I try hard to appreciate the eastern values which direct him. Sadness stomps in and slaps me. This beautiful, perfect man is at war with himself. How does society have the right to do this to a person, I wonder? My sadness exits and tags anger. I want to fight every person who has a problem with Rifqi's sexuality. I want to defend our natural feelings to his religious leaders. I want to help his family to understand. I know it is not my place. I hardly know this man, yet I would defend his honour even now. The minutes seem to pass so slowly. Rifqi turns back to look at me. He attempts to appear calm and composed.

'Rob, you are so sweet and so patient. I am drawn to you by a power I cannot define. But you are... how to say... naive?' I smile inside at the cuteness of his accent but remain composed on account of the seriousness of our conversation.

'Yes, you are probably right, Rifqi. I recognise that. I want a life like that in a romance movie. Swept off my feet by a handsome young man who will do anything to make me happy. In my imaginary life, no one causes us problems and there is no heartache. Hence, why my expectations are never met. It is not real, right? But I know how much I already care and feel for you, and I am willing to try to understand the complexity of your situation.'

Rifqi's signature sexy smile reflects he appreciates the sentiment at least. His heart weighs heavy and his mind is clearly confused but for now, he tries to shake it off. Back on the bike, I take advantage of being "allowed" to move in closer and take the opportunity for a hug. On the opposite side of the road, I am sure that I spot two young males watching us and as

Rifqi races off down the main road towards our hotel for the evening, the two men start to follow.

Chapter Ten

The shower refuses to run warm so I take a deep breath and step under the icy waterfall. The hotel is luxurious and the bathroom fit for a prince. I think briefly about Ali's reaction if he was to see me now. He likes the high life and his number one criteria for the perfect suitor is money, so this would certainly meet his expectations. I am less easily impressed. I have had my share of the prestigious living with Max and it made me miserable. My attraction to Rifqi is almost spiritual. The mystery and complexity of Rifqi make for a perfect cocktail of intrigue. Still so many unknowns. The identity of the pursuers earlier bothers me slightly.

I sense the water finally increase its temperature and simultaneously feel someone step in behind me. The heat rises suddenly as Rifqi's skin presses ever so gently against mine. His distinctive smell cuddles me and my body relaxes. He sniffs the left side of my neck and then the right before breathing heavily into my ear. My knees weaken and my breathing quickens. I feel he is hard as he hugs me tightly before spinning me around to face him. His eyes look different. So sexy, so sultry. He looks determined. I bite on my bottom lip as I take in the view before me. The craftsmanship of his body is incredible. The chest – large and defined with two chocolate drop nipples swelling in anticipation. I place one between my finger and thumb, and caress it delicately. Rifqi's head drops back, revealing the nave of his neck that I perceive as an invitation. I start to kiss slowly: long lingering kisses with the occasional flicker of a tongue. The taste of him equalling the delight of the smell. His moans give me the approval I seek; the throbbing of his cock asks me to continue. I take my lips down a slow path of discovery. Circling my tongue around and across the epicentre of his nipples that are now engorged with excitement; my left hand grabs at his chest whilst the right dances over his abs. He feels incredible. My senses are overwhelmed.

'Haha, glee!' Rifqi chuckles.

'Glee?'

'How do you say in English... tinkerly?'

'Oh ticklish. Haha. Sorry!' I laugh. 'Rifqi, who were those men following us today on the bikes?' I am not sure why I pick this moment to ask such a question.

'Just some messengers I asked to meet me to collect a document. Nothing to worry about.' I sense Rifqi is not being honest with me but the image of Rifqi's naked torso distracts me. I take a step back, pressing myself against the cooler glass that gives me a moment to catch my breath, as I feel myself edging towards my climax. Rifqi looks into my eyes and smiles in a way that only he can. Softly, he places both palms on either side of my face before kissing me. His lips taste of lemon. Fresh and fruity. Full and impeccably soft. I am addicted already. His open lips close on mine and they are a perfect fit, like two halves of a friendship pendant. The pace of each kiss quickens and I feel his tongue brush against mine. A shiver fires down the length of my body; the individual hairs of my entire torso standing to attention. His hands explore my body and run down my back to my buttocks. His movements are slow and soft. His tongue pushes a little more firmly against my mouth so I relax my mouth and part my lips ready to taste him even more. The citrus flavours quench my thirst. My body screams for more as my hands grab at his caramel skin. I *need* more like an addict craving a harder fix.

I drop to my knees, now facing his pulsating phallus. A fine trail of hair descends from his belly button and meets a finely sculpted perimeter of intense black pubic hair. The skin of his circumcised dick is slightly darker and my hunger begs me to satisfy it. Taking him in my mouth, I close my eyes and savour the taste. He hardens even more as his moans refine to groans. The gland of his penis fills my mouth. His pre-cum indicates satisfaction. My left hand runs up along his hairless slim thighs and caress his balls that are now hanging low from the heat of the shower. The water cascades down his body and washes over me. I gently tug at his sack and circle his balls in my palm. Rocking my head back and forth, altering the speed according to the tune of his cries. Seeking more, I slide my hand behind. His butt is hairless, smooth and full. Having not had the conversation about sexual roles, I am unsure of how my next move will be received but I am unable to stop my exploration. My index finger gently circles the ring of his hole. Rifqi flinches slightly and takes a gasp of breath. He does not push me away but rather positions himself more favourably, lifting his leg up and resting his foot on the small ledge inside the cubicle. I press a little harder, and as the tip enters, the muscles contract suddenly and envelope my finger. He feels so warm. So moist. I grab at my own dick from which my pre-cum oozes. Rifqi grabs at my head and pushes himself deep into my mouth almost causing me to gag. My own load releases across the mosaic tiles as I taste him at the back of my throat. The taste slightly acidic yet moorish. Rifqi's legs buckle slightly as he slides down the tiled wall and sits face to face with me.

'That was…'

'Incredible,' Rifqi interrupts. 'I have never been with a guy before.'

'Seriously?' I screech without tact. 'But how? I mean why?'

'It just never seemed right. I told you… it's…'

'Complicated. Right?' I jump in but add a small smile to keep the moment light. 'I think we need to get out of here, my skin is all shrivelled like an old man.' I step out of the shower first and grab one of the luxury white towels hanging on the rail next to the overly large mirror. I catch a glimpse of Rifqi's anguish before he notices me staring and laughs it off.

'Let me dry you,' he requests. Rifqi takes the towel from me, and begins to slowly mop the water from my back and thighs, whilst taking a sneaky feel of my butt.

'Such a good arse,' he chuckles. His movements are so considered, so disciplined. Wrapping both arms around me from behind, he holds me close and whispers, 'I think I am falling for you.'

Chapter Eleven

I wake to the sound of the Bali Mynah and a room drenched in eastern sunlight. Rifqi still sleeps beside me, his arm draped over me. Our contrasting naked flesh entangled. My Mediterranean glow looks so pale in contrast. His slim, smooth legs entwine with my stockier, hairier ones. His breathing is shallow and his lips slightly parted. One day stubble circles his lips only. I am in awe of his beauty both inside and out, and I move in closer for a morning snuggle.

'Back off, Mr!' Rifqi chuckles, as he opens just one eye to check on my position. I force myself between his arms that he has now playfully crossed tightly to keep me away. He crumbles when I slap his buttocks and I jump onto his chest, knocking him flat on his back. I brush back the strands of hair that have fallen unevenly onto his startled face.

'You are just too lovable, Mr Permana.'

'And you are just too handsome, Mr Robbie.'

'Mr Sparks to you, if you please,' I reply as I realise it is probably the first time he has heard my surname. Realisation hits me – there is still so much to learn about each other. Yet it excites me. For the first time in my candid little life, I realise I am excited by an unknown future.

'Can we just stay here for a few months? Just like this,' I ask.

'Oh that would be heavenly, Robbie, but I already plan to return to my home town next week on business, although only for a few days. It was all arranged before I met you and a little difficult to postpone now,' Rifqi's announcement comes out of the blue, and I sense my body clearly tensing though I try to control it and look relaxed.

'Hey, why don't you come with me? I would love to show you around Jogjakarta.'

I feel elated and my ear to ear grin clearly reflects this. Sensing I am blushing, I drop my head upon Rifqi's chest to hide my school boy glow.

'But what about your family? The things you said about them not accepting gay people. How will you explain why I am there?' I query.

'Oh don't overthink that. I will just tell them you are a friend or business associate. It will be fine,' Rifqi replies.

Business associate? How bloody romantic. Sometimes I don't understand this man. One moment his family seem like religious extremists tearing his heart apart, the next, he wants me to meet them.

'One more surprise for you,' Rifqi states.

I am not sure I really want to hear it as my mind is already in overdrive from the previous announcement. 'I have booked a meal for us tonight at *Vibes* in Seminyak. There is a great beach there and we have a private villa,' Rifqi boasts.

'Hopefully with another shower big enough for two,' I interrupt playfully.

'Naughty!' laughs Rifqi.

I recall from Ali that *Vibes* is the biggest hot spot in Bali with waiting lists for bookings stretching over weeks. It's popular with the expat community and high society locals. Few tourists frequent the place, due to the difficulty with securing a reservation. I feel so excited and can't wait to tell Ali, who I know will be so envious.

Rifqi springs from the bed reaching for the robe nearby. Giving me a cheeky grin, he disappears into the bathroom. I quickly send a text message to Kimberly, intentionally making it sound dramatic, *I am SOOOO in love. Miss you xx.* I pull the cotton sheets up to cover my face, and kick my hands and feet with excitement like a child before Christmas. My elation is disturbed by the sudden commencement of a comprehendible conversation coming from the bathroom. I creep to the door and guess from the sole voice that Rifqi is on the phone, and seems very agitated. *Why did I not hear it ring? Why would he have his phone with him in the bathroom?* My mind races once more, spurred on by my insecurities that I constantly drag around with me from place to place, relationship to relationship. It feels so strange to hear him speaking in a different language, each word having no meaning for me. It is as if he has transformed into another person. I long to decode the meaning of this unknown language though I can perceive from the loud tone that he is not happy. I take a step closer and press my ear to the door as it flies open.

'Oops,' I say as I take a short stumble into the doorway.

'I am sorry, Robbie. I should not have taken that call when you are here.'

'Is everything okay?' I ask pressing for information yet trying to look laid back.

'Why is your phone on silent? Why are you carrying your phone around with you?' *Way to go with working the laid back persona, Robbie!* The change in Rifqi's body language and facial expression suggests my inquisition has aggravated him though he avoids the need to berate me.

'Just my family. They are very demanding sometimes. They want me to return to Jogjakarta earlier than planned but I refused, much to the unhappiness of my younger brother,' Rifqi explains.

'So what will you do?' I ask, my anxiety rising in anticipation of disappointment.

'Nothing. I will not have Amat dictate to me. He is my younger brother and should show me more respect.'

'What is the urgency for your returning a few days ahead of schedule?' I question, now fully aware I am pushing.

Rifqi takes a deep breath and takes a seat on the edge of the overly large bath. He presses his hands down on his thighs and drops his head. I take a step forward, and place my fingers on his chin and tilt his head up. He looks upset so I kiss his forehead remembering how soothing I found this gesture in the forest.

'My brother wishes to marry a girl he has fallen in love with,' Rifqi explains with a surprising level of disapproval in his voice considering the good news.

'That's great. So why are you so sad about that? Is she not right for him?' I ask.

'In my culture, siblings marry in order of age. He is my younger brother which means he cannot marry until I do. So my family wants to meet to discuss my plans as their patience with my free-spirit is slowly irritating them,' Rifqi answers before lowering his head as if defeated.

'Oh…' I scramble around to find a string of words to follow but they are AWOL. My mind is racing. *Is Rifqi telling me he is getting married?* But he is gay! I feel irritated. How dare society or a family *force* someone into this situation. 'I am a little confused, Rifqi. Are you actually telling me you plan to get married just so your younger brother can have his wish?' I push.

'NO!' Rifqi bites back before appearing remorseful for snapping in response to a perfectly legitimate question. His body relaxes slightly. 'No. I am not saying I *am* going to get married. I am saying that my family *want* me to get married.'

'Well fuck them, Rifqi!' I retort angrily. 'Only you have the right to decide on your destiny. You are not the property of your family. They can't force you to marry.' A red mist engulfs me but I reflect back to my last encounter with her back in London. I try to calm myself, aware that my own selfish frustrations are only a further burden to Rifqi.

'You don't understand, Robbie. How could you?'

'Try me,' I respond. Deep down, I know I will not comprehend the idiocy of this.

'I come from a predominantly Muslim country. I have already explained the feelings towards homosexuality. My culture is also very traditional. Women there have no comprehension of two men loving each other. They only know a man and a woman. And, of course, on top of that, we are…' Rifqi pauses suddenly. My eyes widen and I nod my head to indicate for him to proceed. Silence. He looks like a naughty pupil holding the broken toy with nowhere to hide.

'*We are*… we are what, Rifqi?' I press gently.

'What?' Rifqi asks, clearly pretending to look puzzled.

'You just said *we are* but then you stopped suddenly. What were you going to say?' Rifqi appears flustered. He licks his lips in a way that Max used to whenever he was building up to a lie. He turns to look away.

'It doesn't matter. I forget now.' The lie fails to fool me. Years of being on the receiving end of countless false truths has perfected my ability to detect one.

I opt for avoiding a confrontation and choose to believe that Rifqi is not a carbon copy of Max. We sit silently for a moment but it feels awkward so I attempt to be proactive and find a solution.

'So why don't you go back home a little earlier and just talk it through with your family? I mean, at least, explain that you are not ready to marry.' I hear how silly my suggestion is but my lips move before my brain catches up. Rifqi smiles. A smile that acknowledges my feeble attempt, yet looks unquestionably patronising.

'I just can't bear to lose you, Rifqi. I know it has all been so quick and maybe it is too soon to ask anything from you but I feel so complete with you. The thought of that being taken away from me frightens me.' I avoid eye contact, fearful my outpouring of love is a little overbearing. Rifqi gives no reply which only further taunts my insecurities. I choose not to be selfish and just give Rifqi the hug he so desperately needs.

We sit side by side on the edge of the bath. No words are spoken. They are not needed. We interlock fingers, and he raises my hand to his lips as if to kiss but gently sniffs and holds my hand next to his heart. I feel his pain and his confusion, yet do not know how to take it away from him.

'What will I do, Robbie? My family demand I marry but I know I am gay and I know I cannot be the husband I need to be. I cannot love my "wife" in the way a man should. I cannot bring children into a marriage that is not built on honesty. Yet, I cannot tell my family the truth,' Rifqi pauses. His pain clearly visible. 'would lose everything and more,' he adds.

I am unable to offer any words of support in response. This is outside of my thinking. I always took my parents disinterest in my coming out for granted. I assumed they did not care as they were too wrapped up in their own affairs but I now realise it was also a blessing. To feel you would lose your family and more for just being yourself is insane for me.

'Maybe your family would understand? Or maybe you can just continue to delay the conversation. Or maybe…' I start to cry as desperation chokes me. I know my words are stupid and impractical. Rifqi appreciates the sentiment, and softly wipes away my tears and kisses me softly. My pain and his turmoil are exchanged. We sit. Each one of us independently thinking through a string of unanswerable questions. Ten minutes or so later, and Rifqi springs to his feet and gives a little wiggle as if to shake off his heavy load. The lack of co-ordination in his "dance" move entertains me and I can't help but laugh at the effort.

'Hey, let's try to forget this for now. Let's go to the beach and enjoy our time together. My family are *my* problem and I am sorry for burdening you.' Deep down, I know the despair that Rifqi feels and even deeper, I know that things are going to become even more complex for us both. For now, I *try* to just enjoy the moment. Something that certainly does not come naturally to me.

Chapter Twelve

Outside the hotel sits Wahyu in a black Mercedes waiting for us to climb in. He is sporting a new pair of black shades, resembling no other personal assistant I have previously encountered. The Bluetooth ear piece that sits in his left ear intermittently flashes. He seems to provide a running commentary of our journey, along with constantly refreshed ETAs. The short 30-minute drive to the coastal region of Nusa Dua seems much longer when conducted in silence. I sense Rifqi is distracted by his early morning dispute with his brother, though he paints a somewhat fake smile across his handsome face.

For the third time, I take a deep inhale of breath as if to absorb every possible ounce of courage to ask some questions. I am not afraid of Rifqi though fearful my questioning will be perceived as prying.

'Have you ever... been with a girl?' I coyly ask. Rifqi laughs, though seems bemused. Wahyu glares back at us in the rear view mirror. *Does he know the truth, I wonder?*

'Have *you*?' he volleys back.

'You cannot answer a question with a question, Rif.' I notice how I have shortened his name and wonder if anyone has ever called him this or if I can claim this sign of endearment as my own.

'Let's talk about this later, Robbie, we have a beautiful beach calling to us!'

I know from years of dealing with Max's antics that this is a diversion tactic. My head drops slightly as my mind begins to race. Rifqi places a firm hand on my left shoulder – a sign of reassurance, I wonder?

Wahyu pulls up to an entrance that reminds me of a gated compound, and the lone security guard scans the wheel arches and chassis with a metal detector.

'It's okay,' smiles Wahyu, who has clearly seen my concern as he glances back. 'It is normal now since those terrible bombings in Bali back in 2002.'

The resort screams extravagance. A crescent of private beach villas, each hidden inside a perimeter of high foliage, frame an isolated beach that is reserved for guests only. There is enough distance from the hotels that flank us on either side not to distract. It is hopelessly romantic.

Stepping out of the car, Wahyu signals for the staff, each wearing traditional Balinese clothing, to escort us to the villa entrance whilst a small team of suited men empty the car. One looks familiar. At first, I just assume his striking looks capture my attention but there is something about his eyes. I squint a little, trying to focus and then it hits me. He was one of the men near Monkey Forest who was watching us from a short distance and followed us as we rode off. Our apparent stalker appears uncomfortable with my scrutiny and scurries off with our belongings.

'Rifqi, that man was following us before. I remember him.'

'Haha, that's Kris. He works for me,' replies Rifqi, simply brushing it off.

'You know, I don't think you have really explained your line of business,' I frankly state.

'I already told you – import and export. Nothing exciting.' *More mystery in his generic responses.* 'Now take a look inside in here and tell me you are not impressed.' Rifqi seems proud and his massive grin releases my obsession with the constant mystery that surrounds him.

As we climb two or three stone steps and pass through an archway, a large private pool greets us. A large spacious gazebo draped in white cloth and housing a large comfortable mattress sits to the right. Two sun loungers wait patiently for us with a thirst-quenching mocktail already prepared on the adjacent side tables. The sizable villa sits quietly behind. An expanse of glass folding doors dress the entire front of the property. The large, open plan living space is immaculately dressed. White Italian tiles reflect the sunlight and contrast beautifully with the black marble kitchen worktop. My attention is diverted to two young locals busy preparing in the kitchen.

'Private chefs?' I ask.

'Of course,' smiles Rifqi. 'Only the best for you.'

Rifqi babbles away in his native tongue and the staff all disperse, leaving an impressive buffet lunch for us to savour after a quick dip in the refreshing cool water of the pool.

After way too much food, we step out onto the beach that sits at the foot of the bedroom terrace to the rear of the property. The white sand feels like talc between my toes and the palm tree backdrop completes the idyllic image. The pristine floor is littered only with a few broken coconut shells, and leaves that the sapphire waters wash over and transport out to sea. The beach is unusually deserted and I briefly wonder where the guests of the other five villas are. The staff seem overly attentive, reminding me of the night we first met at *The Cage*. I decide to challenge Rifqi on the ever present entourage who continue to follow us but lose my focus and my breath as Rifqi strips to a dazzling pair of red speedos in a flash, and playfully bounds to the water, calling after me. The swimwear hugs his pert bottom, and his legs look longer and more slender. As Rifqi spins around to check on my progress, he tumbles backwards and falls under the waves. Emerging seconds later in a dramatic flap, I fall to my knees in hysterics. His black hair pressed to his forehead covers his vision slightly and his gaping mouth fights for breath like a new born. Stood in the shallow water, the sun beaming across his torso, I cannot help but freeze in admiration of his beauty. As he pushes back his hair, his biceps contract and his abs tighten. I feel the need to cover my less impressive body. Rifqi extends his arm to call me into the soothing water away from the intense heat.

Bobbing about in the water, Rifqi maintains some distance between us and seems overly aware of the staff stood near our villa. Wahyu seems to be pacing and of course, continues to communicate via Bluetooth. *Who he is speaking to? A lover? More staff? His family?* We talk about my family, my coming out and my father's obsession with women before I decide to return to our earlier conversation. 'Tell me, Mr Permana, have your ever dated or had sex with the female species?' My formality is an attempt to keep things light-hearted.

'Well, in high school, I had some female friends. And some of them asked me to be their boyfriend.'

And…?' I push further.

'And what?' Rifqi looks genuinely confused by my further questioning for detail.

'Did you kiss? Or more…'

'I tried to kiss one of them but…' Rifqi stops.

'But what?' My eagerness for detail worries me.

'To be honest, I found it… how to say? Um… disgusting!'

We both break out into uncontrollable giggles as a larger wave washes over us and entangles our bodies. For just a moment, we are entwined and it seems as though the ocean has paused. Our eyes connect and I feel something so deep inside. An ecstatic wave of excitement that is difficult to contain. In an instant, we return to real time, and Rifqi takes a step back and looks across to his "staff" beckoning us to return to shore as the sun's descent to bed speeds up.

As Rifqi scrambles out of the water, I grab his arm as my curiosity does not feel satisfied.

'So you have never had sex with a girl?'

'No!' The answer is short and direct. 'You forget, Robbie. This is not the west. Attitude towards sex is different, especially in Muslim families. It is not acceptable to have sex outside of marriage.'

I feel somewhat naive as I realise I continue to completely overlook the cultural and religious differences that stand between us. My questions are so ingrained in western values. I recognise the need to bury this topic right in the sand beneath my feet. The falling sun burns a glorious shade of red then stops me in my tracks. As I catch up with Rifqi, I am caught off guard by Wahyu who looks serious as he talks into Rifqi's ear. It seems a little unusual to me that someone would have their Personal Assistant on standby at the beach but as I cannot afford such a luxury, I brush it off due to my own ignorance. It does baffle me why such a hench-looking guy would work in a role requiring such attention to detail. As the two part ways from their whispering huddle, Rifqi seems somewhat troubled.

'Is everything okay, Rif?'

'Yes, all is fine. My mother has requested that I return to Jogjakarta tomorrow. Seems Amat felt the need to involve her since I would not take direct instruction from him. I cannot, of course, ignore my mother's wishes as that would be both inappropriate and disrespectful,' Rifqi appears to be babbling but I appreciate his effort to explain.

'Will you join?' he asks.

'I would be honoured,' I squeal with uncontrollable excitement.

A quick shower and we stroll down the steps of the villa to an idyllic dinner on the moonlit beach front. Ribbons of white light dance across the waves that seem to be in slow motion. As they lick the sand, the sound provides a hushed ambience. A single table nestles on the sand. A bottle of something enticing sits in a silver bucket to the side. The romanticism steals my breath and I cannot contain my emotion. My eyes well and I stop to enjoy the gesture. All of my life, I have longed for this kind of love: this level of appreciation for a significant other. And now it is here, stood in front of me. Rifqi stands silently, grinning: bewitching me with his alluring black eyes that shimmer like glassy onyx. His linen shirt bellows in the gentle breeze revealing the sun-kissed skin of his naval.

A beautiful young Balinese girl approaches the table, and bows her head in respect before pouring a glass of bubbly for us both and placing the crisp white napkins on our laps. She appears a little shy and embarrassed. Based on Rifqi's description of the naivety of Indonesian women, I wonder if she is aware of the nature of our relationship. As we raise a toast to good friendship and love, two young men bring our first plate of heaven. The cuter one of the two takes a sly glance from the corner of his eye and noticing me smiling, he gives a quick smile in return. My gay-dar flashes briefly and I consider if he endures the same struggles as my companion opposite me. The food is exquisite – the perfect Indo-European fusion. Neither of us feels the need to speak. The food consumes our senses. We simply gaze at each other. The intensity of his stare intimidates me and I look away grinning. Rifqi wraps his bare feet around my legs. His playful gesture astounds me. I return my gaze and bite on my bottom lip. My desires are rising rapidly. The sand, sea and food are turning me on, and I long for the opportunity to make love to Rifqi right on this spot. When my handsome waiters return with the second course, I am brought back to reality and my erect cock once again returns to sleep. *Be patient, Mr.*

'This food is insanely good,' I say as I take my second mouthful of the tender beef that is dressed in a spicy peanut coating. 'The flavours are just so intense, yet perfectly balanced.'

'I think you are very passionate about food,' laughs Rifqi. 'I can see where that passion in the bedroom comes from. I need to learn to cook to keep you interested.''

'I would never lose interest in you, Mr.' I blush with embarrassment at how cheesy my comment sounds, though I know it is the truth. I cannot put into words the feelings swirling around my soul. They run incredibly deep and wash over me in waves. It is peaceful, yet electrifying. It feels safe, yet daring. Just ten days ago, I felt my life was hopeless when the reality of my life with Max struck my face hard. I never imagined in such a short time, I would be feeling this way with someone else. Let alone someone so amazing.

'Tell me why you came to Indonesian, Robbie?' Rifqi asks suddenly.

The question was not anticipated and I lose my composure slightly. Images of Max flood my memory, ending with the final snapshot of his lover bleeding on *my* floor. I consider Max. What is he doing now? How did he respond to my disappearance? I long to hate him for what he made me witness but the hate surprisingly does not come.

'Robbie? Are you okay? I did not mean to push you. I was just interested to know how you came to be here.'

Shake it off, Robbie, for Christ's sake. Max broke your heart or have you forgotten that now?

'I um... well... I realised that my life was not what I thought it was and I needed to make a change, a really big change in order to take control.' I am confused as to why I have opted to speak in riddles. There seems no logic in omitting the details of Max but I am concerned it is still too raw and if any emotion is shown, it may scare Rifqi away. Rifqi holds my gaze, most likely still hungry for more information. His eyes widen as if to say *'go on'* but I opt for playing dumb instead. A few minutes pass in silence and I consider whether Rifqi will push for more information. It troubles me why I am not willing to talk about the circumstances that led me to be in Bali. Part of me is ashamed of what happened at the apartment, part is embarrassed about what it says about my character, to have put up with Max's antics for so long. Perhaps, sensing my reluctance to share more at this point, Rifqi begins to speak and changes the direction of his questioning.

'So what will you do for work? I assume, you intend to stay for a while?' he asks.

'My good friend Ali is trying to line up some IT work for me. Then I can get my own place and start the rest of my life.'

'Room for me in that new life of yours?' jokes Rifqi playfully.

We take a stroll along the water edge, the moonlight guiding the way. Wahyu attempts to follow like an obedient puppy but Rifqi signals for him to retreat. The water gently splashes at our ankles, wetting our trousers slightly. I close my eyes and absorb every moment, yet the images of Max return to taunt me. It makes no sense why now I would waste this moment thinking of him. *You don't forget that many years with someone so quickly, Robbie. Be realistic!* Slender fingers slide in between mine and my hand sits inside another's. I open my eyes smiling yet I see Max smiling back at me. My smile is immediately wiped away. I know the image of Max is nothing more than a mirage in the water.

'Are you okay?' The sound of Rifqi's voice shakes me from the illusion. Max has gone and instead Rifqi stands beside me. The darkness hides us and so I throw myself into his arms, relieved by the reality. I tilt my head back and feel a sense of awe at the night sky that is sprinkled with so many stars shining down on us. It is so rare to see such a black sky away from the lights of bustling cities. Rifqi moves closer and ever so gently places his lips on the nave of my neck. The moment is perfect as we stroll back to our table for dessert.

A three course gourmet sensation and a bottle of something clearly expensive, and we tumble onto the bed, back in the total privacy of our villa. All the staff, including Wahyu, have been dismissed and released of their duties. It's me, my man and a sexual craving that needs to be satisfied. Rifqi rests his weary head on my chest. I feel my shaft begin to pulsate on his thigh. Tilting his head back slightly, Rifqi parts his lips – an invitation I assume and I lean in for a kiss. The pace is slow. Our eyes fixed on one another and at this time, I feel like the centre of his universe. I flick my tongue across his top lip and instantly there is movement in his groin. Repositioning myself, I straddle Rifqi, and unbutton his crisp white shirt to reveal flesh so pure and so unspoilt. My hands grab at the pectoral muscles that twitch and tighten with every movement Rifqi makes. His hand slides down the rear of my linen pants and I tense slightly as his soft fingers brush across the rim.

'Suck my nipple,' he breathlessly demands and I feel a duty to oblige. Slow, quick, slow, quick. Soft, hard, soft, hard. I alternate the pace, force whipping Rifqi into a frenzy. His legs kick out beneath me and his toes curl in delight.

'You are so good at this,' he exhales. His fingers now press with greater force and his index finger slips slowly inside, stealing my breath for a moment. A brief shard of pain disperses quickly and waves of ecstasy take over as he slowly moves his hand in small yet incredibly pleasurable circles.

I slide down his body forcing him to release his hold and unzip his trousers. His erection waits patiently to be released as I nibble at his white briefs, consumed by the manly scent that he emits. Releasing him, I wrap my fingers around the shaft and take him in my mouth, flickering my tongue along the length. His cock swells with excitement and his balls tighten and nestle close to his body. He raises his legs and rolls his hips enabling me to take him deeper. The taste of his pre-cum drives me wild and I long to feel the full force of his load deep in my throat.

'I want to make love to you, Robbie. I want to feel what it's like to be inside you. To make our bodies one.' These are the only words of persuasion I need to hear and so I spring back to his moist lips to reconnect us. His cheeks look flushed and small pellets of sweat form across his forehead. I hold his gaze and he smiles back lustfully. His eyes are different. Blacker. More determined. Sexier if that is possible. His breaths are shallow and the short inhales contract his abs that I run my hand along. So impressive to the touch and so exciting to the eye. Rifqi's hand slides down the side of my body; his eyes still gazing so deep into my soul. He wraps his slender fingers around my pulsating cock and bites his lower lip as he slowly yet assertively strokes my gland.

'That feels *so* good. Oh my god! Too good. Stop!' I cry out as a wave of ecstasy almost smothers me.

'Haha, you like that, don't you?' jests Rifqi as he unhurriedly drops his hand down below my balls and slide his palm back towards the rim. 'I want to make love to you,' he begs. 'But I don't want to hurt you.'

'You won't,' I exhale, as I pass the lube to him whilst negotiating the condom down his roaring erection. He delicately inserts a silky finger deep inside me, reaching the spot quickly that swells in anticipation. As he stretches me with an additional finger, I close my eyes to focus on the pleasure and the intimacy of the moment. My brain is in lock-down. Any questions have stopped. My worries and anxieties are at rest. I just swim in a sea of erogenous emotions. I cannot wait any longer and so align myself above his muscular frame. Placing my palms on his sculpted chest, I lower myself onto him. The pain is too much and I elevate myself slightly. I catch his gaze and I fall. Fall deep inside his soul. I love this man so much and I need to feel connected as one. The stretch is almost unbearable yet electrifying as my spine pulsates from one end to another. My neurones are overwhelmed, my senses in overdrive. Slowly, I rock my hips, each movement taking Rifqi deeper inside me. Sweat dapples his chest. I lean forward and kiss him so deep, so rough. The taste like nectar. His pulls gently on the back of my hair with his left hand and uses the right to rock me faster. Harder. Rifqi begins to pant. I know he is about to climax so I disconnect our bodies quickly.

'Slow down, Mr Permana. I am not done with you yet.' Without warning, Rifqi throws me onto my back. He looks possessed. He clearly needs to release and it excites me tremendously. My own cock leaks with a desire so deep. A sharp pain distracts me as Rifqi pushes deep inside me. His eyes never leaving mine. Sweat flies from his hair and onto my chest. His guns locked and loaded. The impressive definition of his arms as he props himself up, accelerates my journey to climax. My hands grab and stroke his chest. His abs. His face. I cannot hold any longer as waves of elation release onto my stomach and chest. Simultaneously, I feel the weight of Rifqi on my own body as his legs spasm and his arms give way. His breathing is heavy in the nave of my neck. Even his heavy breathing is so enticing. We cling to one another wrapped in new emotions, new sensations and new experiences.

'Well, considering that was your first time, I am a little lost for words,' I mock.

'That's a first for you also then,' giggles Rifqi as he pulls me in closer for a hug that seems to last a lifetime.

Chapter Thirteen

Touching down at Adisucipto International Airport, I feel incredibly excited to be meeting Rifqi's family. Though only a one-hour flight, Rifqi found the time to give me the run down on his family. It was the first time I realised that his father had, sadly, passed away in the previous year. We glided over the topic yet I saw the sadness in his eyes. I was anticipating a set of rules on how I should conduct myself on account of the family being unaware of Rifqi's sexual preferences, but these never came. I guess the lack of English will provide a natural divide between us in which things can be miscommunicated and misunderstood.

The arrivals "lounge" is definitely cute. I am sure the same guy who was directing the airplane into the bay is now running back and forth to the aircraft, luggage in tow, probably weighing twice his body weight. No conveyor belts in sight, just a wooden rail on which the bags sit waiting to be claimed. The constant staring from others would have made me incredibly paranoid, had Rifqi not explained the local fascination with white folk. The request for selfies certainly makes me feel like a celeb. One of the greatest things about small airports – no queues. Four steps forward after collecting our bags and we were out into the arrivals hall, or should I say room.

'Apa kapar?' Words I do not understand.

'Baik Baik.' More mysterious words. But from the ritualistic sniffing, I assume this is Rifqi's family. A little unexpected as I thought Rifqi had arranged a car. *Had I known, I would have freshened up a little.* I briefly wonder how we will all fit in the car with so many of them here to greet us. *Us?* I realise now that they are unaware of my presence: stood grinning like an idiot in the background. I give Rifqi a gentle nudge from behind. A reminder of my existence and feeling of awkwardness.

'Ah, Robbie, come and say hello to my mother.'

'Ibu, ini, Robbie.' I stand there, still smiling.

'Selamat pagi.' Two words. Two firm, unemotional, unfriendly words. An icy scowl accompanies the welcome. Rifqi's mother is a tiny lady, both in height and weight, and clearly holds the key to the beauty that was passed on to her son. She wears an elegant lime headscarf which is beautifully embroidered in gold thread. To the left of her stands a rather angry looking guy, not too dissimilar looking from Rifqi, so I make the assumption that it is Amat: the younger brother. A heated exchange of words takes place between siblings so I try to look invisible and fade into the diminishing crowds, and observe my surroundings. The airport is very traditional with wooden exposed beams and beautiful carvings. There is no air con so the air is warm and humid. The choking atmosphere is not helped by the large number of older men smoking in every corner. It is a sight I have only a distant memory of in London following the ban on smoking in public places. Clearly, no such laws here.

'Why are *you* here?' A firm, slightly antagonised question flies my way from Amat, before Rifqi intercepts.

'How dare you speak to my guest in that way. Robbie is with me. He is a good friend from Bali and I want to show him my hometown. Is that okay with you?'

Amat barely looks at me. He just picks up my luggage and hurries everyone outside to the car.

'Selamat datang, Robbie,' a gentle voice calls over my shoulder. I turn and see the absolute image of Rifqi in a female form. She is beauty defined. Tall, slender and a face of porcelain that is perfectly framed with her cropped black hair. Her incredibly large eyes are friendly and warm, yet I sense her shyness.

'This is my sister Annisa. She looks after me and keeps Amat in check,' laughs Rifqi as he links arms with his older sister.

'Apa?' responds a puzzled Annisa.

'She does not speak much English, I am afraid. But she has not stopped smiling so she likes you for sure,' Rifqi explains.

'Well, one out of three is not bad,' I jest as we squeeze into the car. Unable to partake in the dialogue, I watch the world of Jogjakarta pass by. The city, located on the island of Java, is a jewel of tradition, arts and culture. The complimentary in-flight magazine provided a very useful insight into the city of Jogjakarta. My brief research revealed that the city still has a reigning Sultan who resides at the Royal Palace located inside the grand eighteenth century royal complex or Kraton, as it is more commonly known. We pass a number of open air pavilions which function as living culture museums showcasing exquisite Javanese dance and music shows.

The traffic is light which offers a welcomed surprise as the short 6 kilometre journey comes to an end and we pull into an expansive driveway greeted by a large crowd of what I assume are other family members. The reception is incredible. So many smiles and giggles, and although we have no common language, I am made to feel like a VIP. Rifqi's two nephews and niece stand behind Annisa wary of the unknown visitor. An elderly gentleman extends a hand and as I shake, he places his second hand over mine forming a warm cocoon as he grins continuously at me.

'This is my uncle. He was married to my father's sister but sadly she passed away recently. He lives in one of the houses here in the compound with his two sons,' explains Rifqi.

A collection of other people look more like staff as they stand away at a fixed distance and no one appears to be interacting with them. Stood in the centre of the driveway, I grasp the size of the area. Three large houses stand around the perimeter with a central building that appears to be some kind of function or meeting room. I have so many questions I wish to ask my hosts but I am whisked away to the larger of the three houses by one of the silent extras. My silent guide directs me with hand gestures and smiles only. It is unclear if this is a relative or an employee. The worn, tired clothing would suggest the latter. The house is the epitome of Javanese tradition. The large, wooden entrance doors are intricately carved as are the wooden shutters located on either side. Tiled flooring helps to keep the temperature down. Expansive, elaborate teak furniture

67

outlines the perimeter of the main room. It feels like a trip back in time that has no comparison to my apartment back in London. I scan each room but find no signs of modern technology. Central ceiling fans above creek but do little to prevent the beads of sweat running down my back. My search for air con fails. A small portrait painting hangs in front of me inside the most magnificently carved wooden frame. A grandiose gentleman stands proud whilst two young boys and one little girl surround him. Surprisingly, no one is smiling. It all looks rather formal and I do not recognise anyone.

The waving hand signals my room to the left I assume which thankfully, has an en-suite bathroom to the side. As I step into adjacent room, I gasp at the sight of the traditional shower – a barrel of cold water and a small bucket. My outburst of shock makes the timid young lady giggle as she quickly exits my room. Despite feeling a little grubby, I put off the icy initiation and rest on the edge of my bed. A gentle tap on the door and Rifqi steps in.

'Hey, is the room okay for you?'

'The room is lovely,' I gratefully reply. 'The shower... well... that will take a bit of getting used to.' Rifqi just laughs and falls back on to the bed. I lean down to give him a kiss but he springs forward with horror on his face.

'No! Robbie, I told you about this. For three days, you are my good friend from Bali and nothing more. Please respect the difficulty of my situation.'

I lower my head, 'Sorry.'

Rifqi gently taps my knee, gives a wide grin to reassure me. 'We will go for dinner soon. Take a rest for now whilst I catch up with everyone,' states Rifqi and then he exits. I feel my phone vibrate and so take it out to reveal a message from Ali that reads: *Hope you are having as much sex as I am. Oh and get some sun on that pale skin. Miss you! X.*

Ali's message makes me chuckle and I realise I miss him too. I have so much to be grateful to him for. I would have still been stuck in London, alone and miserable if it were not for his generous offer. I need to spend more time with him when I return. My thoughts are interrupted by the door creaking open. I assume Rifqi has returned to summons me to shower. Coyly looking up, my smirk is wiped off my face by a sinister looking Amat who steps in and slowly closes the door behind him.

'Stay away from brother. He need marry girl not stay with men like you.' Despite the broken English, the words were no less cutting. *Men like me??* What did that mean? Foreigners…? GAY!! Did he actually mean gay? I cannot gather my thoughts quickly enough to respond. They race around and around in my mind. I am left feeling winded as Amat is already out of the door, leaving me floundering in my surprise. How could his brother possibly sense that I was gay? Does he, therefore, know his brother is also gay and is trying to keep us apart? I feel helpless yet outraged. I contemplate marching down the corridor after him and demanding he justify his antagonism towards me. I reflect on the cold welcome at the airport but had assumed this was for his brother on account of their previous dispute. Helplessness turns to anger. What gives him the right to warn me away from his brother? I pick up my phone and consider calling Ali to ask for his advice but know that Ali will only get equally angry, and in turn, this will fuel my own negative feelings. I now feel uncomfortable staying here and try to think of a plan on how I can check into a hotel, and explain this to Rifqi. The last thing I want is to add to his worries. I sit on the edge of the bed and just pause for a moment. I decide it best to try to brush it off and begin to unpack a few of my clothes when I hear Rifqi shout up the corridor. 'Robbie, take a shower, we will go for dinner in an hour.'

Stood timid and naked in the bathroom, Amat's words continue to bother me. I throw a bucket of chilly water over my chest as a gentle introduction. My body instantly tenses and my balls run for cover. Each arctic droplet takes a slow, cold ride down my body, causing each individual body hair to stand to attention. Recognising the failure in my technique, I grab a second bucket and throw it over my head to fully submerge myself. As the water hits my spine, I gasp for breath before bursting out in laughter. Two buckets later, and I am fully acclimatised and kind of enjoying my little bit of tradition, though I do not linger too long, opting for a quick wash and go.

We arrive at the restaurant and something tells me that we are being watched by a large number of diners. However, remembering the interest in foreigners, I assume it due to my white face. The staff seem particularly attentive as they escort us in large numbers to what appears to be a more private area of the eatery.

'Hey, Rifqi,' I whisper. 'Why are the staff so attentive and why is everyone showing us so much respect?'

'We come here many times. The owner was friends with my Pap.'

Seems logical, right? Amat makes a quick dash to the opposite end of the table, maintaining the furthest possible distance from me, yet never taking his eyes off me. Luckily, I sit next to Annisa and her three children but close enough to Rifqi to have him translate when all else fails.

'Padang food. I from Padang,' states Rifqi's mother proudly. I see the hint of a smile and wonder if she is warming to me but when the scowl returns shortly after, I think twice. The family chat away, giggling and laughing about topics I cannot access, though Rifqi does his best to keep me in the loop by translating the main points. I try out my limited Indonesian phrases on Annisa's eldest son, Rio. No joy. The quizzical stare says it all. I switch to English, assuming that at 14, he would know some familiar phrases. No joy. We both settle for a simple smile as the awkward atmosphere is lifted by the arrival of our meal. Countless small plates are laid out in the centre, each hosting an unfamiliar delicacy I cannot register. As the waitress adds a small ball of rice to my plate, I feel relieved that I will not starve tonight.

'Please start, Robbie,' says Rifqi as he gives me a cheeky grin and a sexy wink. My eyes widen as I look back across the table at Rifqi, trying to explain that I have no cutlery to use. My attempt at charades gives Rifqi the information he needs to understand as he laughs out loud and signals for me to observe the others. Clearly, there is not a knife and folk in sight, and I realise I am to use my hands only. I survey my companions and scrutinise their technique. A small pellet of rice is squashed into a ball then dipped into the leafy dish followed by some crispy chicken. *Well, I am assuming this is chicken.* The taste is incredible. My taste buds are in overdrive trying to decipher the complex new flavours. I scan across the other plates with my newfound confidence for Padang food. Two plates capture my attention. I tilt my head to the side to view from all angles. It looks... familiar. I frown trying to make sense of the shape and unusual texture. My eyes widen, and my mouth drops causing Annisa and her younger son, Henry, to break out into hysterics as they point at the sides of their heads. Brain! My God, there is a brain on the plate and I feel my stomach wrench slightly. It is small and perfectly formed, and I wonder from which animal it was extracted. The horror is clearly expressed on my face despite not wanting to offend my hosts. Even Amat is striking a small grin though probably from enjoying watching me flounder. My appetite continues to plummet as I notice the chicken feet pointing their toes at me. I force a few more balls of rice and vegetables down to avoid any unwelcome attention. Sensing a small tugging at my shirt, I look behind to see Sari beckoning me to follow her. The youngest of Annisa's children, she is the image of her mother. Surprisingly, she holds out a hand to place inside mine and starts to parade me around the restaurant with such pride on her face. She invites a couple at one table to take a picture of me. It is a bizarre experience but the cuteness of Sari is too much. Three photos later, and we are outside in the small garden where a larger group of teens are chatting and drinking milkshakes. Sari beckons them over and they seem only too happy to strike a pose with me. A little five-year-old with the confidence to command everyone's attention. She is definitely Rifqi's niece. Each teenager practices saying *thank you* and *nice to meet you* which I find so endearing.

I take Sari's hand and we walk along the winding path between the slightly overgrown bushes. Amat suddenly steps out, says something to Sari in Indonesian and she rushes off, leaving an atmosphere so tense you can hear the mosquitoes feasting on my flesh.

'I tell you to go home. Rifqi marry woman soon. Because I need to marry my lady.' Amat takes a step closer. We are now nose to nose and I feel his spicy breath on my face. His eyes widen and I see his hate towards me reflecting back. 'I know you are a gay and you want my brother. BUT HE MARRY LADY, OKAY!' The final five words are emphasised and shouted. I do not feel intimidated by Amat. He is shorter than I am and although incredibly lean, I doubt he can punch with much power. Still, his words upset me and I feel the situation is impossible. I lower my head in preparation for accepting defeat as Amat smugly walks away. I am left stunned by the realisation that Amat really does understand his brother's impossible situation and yet encourages his turmoil with his insistence on living a more socially acceptable lifestyle. Images of Rifqi rush through my mind and my heart feels heavy. Heavy with love. I cannot let him go, whatever the family's feelings are towards me. I chase after Amat. Hearing me coming from behind, he spins around. I take a deep breath, push back my shoulders to enlarge my chest and shove my face right into Amat's space.

'I don't care what *you* feel about me. I only care about what your brother feels. And until *he* asks me to leave, I am going nowhere. Now fuck off, take that stick from up your arse and lighten up.' I knew my last phrase would be totally lost in translation. I said it for my own pleasure. I felt so proud for taking a stand. All of my life, I have allowed others to push me about. Anything for an easy life, but now was the time to take a stand.

Returning to the restaurant, Rifqi raises an eyebrow – a question not spoken but still understood. I nod my head and beam a smile back at him. 'Bring on the next gourmet surprise!' I joke.

Chapter Fourteen

The call to prayer at sunrise stirs me from what has been a restless night. I had considered telling Rifqi about my encounter with his brother but did not want to add fuel to the fire that was already igniting between the siblings. I spent the night reflecting back on my life and questioning why it has always been so difficult to just find my slice of happiness. I reminisce briefly about my parents but this is cut short by my anger towards them. The only contact since I left London – a two-word email: *Have fun!* Short, sweet and without the slightest bit of interest as to why I had fled London, and abandoned Max. *And what about Max? Do you miss Max?* I do not allow myself to think about Max. The attentiveness that Rifqi has shown in such a short time surpasses the years of waiting for Max to step up. Images of the blood spilling from his latest twink haunt me briefly. I feel remorse for hurting someone. Someone relatively innocent. Self-pity creeps in. *Why are you so determined to be unhappy, Robbie?*

Another quick breath-taking shower, some rice and fish for breakfast, and we are all crammed in to the car again for our day trip to the Borobudur temple complex in Central Java. Rifqi's mother turns and smiles from the front passenger seat when she sees my face pressed into the side window. I empathise with the construction workers passing by jammed into the open backed trucks. I never imagined it possible to squeeze five people into the back of a saloon, and I am only thankful that Rio has opted to spend the day with a friend and not with us.

Rifqi's mother attempts to make conversation with me but words fail her. Rifqi tried to justify that her apparent previous disinterest was only from a lack of experience in dealing with foreigners. Personally, I wonder if she also senses my true feelings for her son. After all, a mother always knows her own son. Whether she chooses to accept it or not is another matter. Seeing Rifqi so happy, maybe she is grateful for the friendship we share. Nevertheless, I am touched by the sentiment shown. Annisa continues to just grin at me. Her spirit is warm and comforting. She makes me feel at ease without the need to talk. Sari sits on Annisa's lap nodding off from time to time whilst Henry (sandwiched between Rifqi and I) is engrossed with the iPhone that I have given to him to play with.

Noticing my interaction with and fondness for Annisa's children, Rifqi's mum spins around in her seat, and proceeds to blurt out, 'No father. Bad man,' through slightly gritted teeth. I am a little surprised by the words as I had wrongly assumed the husband was working away from home. No one has previously mentioned the children's father. Annisa is thankfully unaware of her mother's words. She just continues to stare innocently into the distance. 'He go work in Vietnam and not come back.' Rifqi glares at his mother with wide eyes. So much communication going on yet with no actual words. His mother retreats, offering me a local snack and turns back in her seat. Rifqi looks at me and shakes his head but I have to admit, I am a little lost in the story though touched by how defensive Rifqi is of his sister.

Amat stares back at me continuously from the rear view mirror as he negotiates the scenic route to our destination. I try to understand him. The social and religious values in which he is submersed are a stark contrast to my western, more liberal ones. I consider that maybe it is not hatred he feels but fear. Fear for his brother and maybe how others would treat him if he was to be true to himself. Or maybe his fears span wider to the family. What would others say about the family if Rifqi was out and proud? Is such a traditional city ready for such a revelation?

Rifqi's mother catches my eye in the side mirror a few times. She grins, making me feel more at ease but I can't help but think she is trying to assess me and my intentions. There is something in her eyes that tells me she has so many questions to ask, if only she had the language. She mumbles some words to Amat who, in turn, fixes his stare on me in the rear view mirror as he translates, 'My mother ask if you have wife?' A random question thrown out there by Rifqi's mother and everyone in the car holds their breath. I am a little lost for words. Amat's eyes are glued to me despite the high speed driving. I look across to Rifqi who is nervously smiling and yet failing to give direction on how best to answer. I momentarily wonder if she is trying to line me up as a substitute to Annisa's AWOL husband.

'Um... I... um... No, Mrs Permana, I do not have a wife. Can you find me one?' I opt for humour. Silence. The silence extents and I shuffle nervously in my seat. Everyone burst outs laughing. I am not sure if it is my attempt at humour but I join in.

'We are laughing because you called my mother Mrs Permana,' chuckles Rifqi.

Rifqi's mother continues to giggle from the front seat, wiping away tears. I am left puzzled. 'In Indonesia, we do not have the same family name like you do in the west. We all have different... how do you say? Second names?' explains Rifqi

'Surnames,' I correct.

'Ah, yes, surnames. In fact, my mother only has one name – Rahmawati, so this is the first time someone has called her Mrs Permana. It's funny for Indonesians.' Rifqi leans across Henry and whispers, 'And that was a perfect technique for avoiding the question she asked you, by the way.'

The journey continues with endless giggles and laughs, and although I still feel like an outsider, I am content in my unfamiliar setting. The sun beams across the paddy fields that stretch as far as the eye can see. Tiny distant figures can be seen working amongst the crops and groups of small bare footed children play nearby. One little boy, no older than Sari ,chases after the rest of his group, waving a large bamboo stick. The clothes are dusty and over-sized, and the skin is incredibly sun-kissed, a stark contrast to Sari's pale skin. As we pass through the village of Wanurejo, the roads distort into narrower dirt tracks. We pass a number of local homes, small one storey houses with tiled roofs, and traditional wooden doors and window frames. Groups of women sit in small circles chatting and preparing food, the smell of which diffuses into the car causing my belly to rumble. I wonder what the conversations are about. Local village gossip, perhaps, in the same way that ladies in a hair salon share stories. Moans and groans about their men, the endless list of household chores to be done or maybe something more exciting like a new love affair. I humour myself briefly before brushing the ideas aside.

Amat pulls over to the side of a road in a small village known as Wanurejo where a local farmer is selling a selection of fruits and vegetables in front of a picturesque backdrop of elegant coconut palms. Everyone exits the car providing a much needed leg stretch. Nearby the stall, a group of four mischievous boys play with a broken deserted wooden boat. Their thick, black hair has been chopped by an amateur barber, most likely a parent. It does not detract from their adorable faces. Dirt smeared mouths with crooked smiles beam at us.

'Selamat pagi,' I gingerly say.

Their eyes widen, surprised by the white man speaking in familiar words. The two youngest giggle hysterically. A more serious looking, slightly older child crouches down on the ground playing with strands of dry grass, looking completely disinterested in my presence. They all wear a mismatch of ill-fitting clothes which look like they have been passed down the family line many times. I am not sure if they are brothers or just friends from the same village. The two gigglers definitely have a striking resemblance. Some unknown words are exchanged between the boys, and they are clambering and jumping from the boat. The show reminds me of our recent trip to Monkey Forest in Ubud. I ask Rifqi to buy some fruit for my new friends and take a quick picture with them to add to the memories. Two of them rest against me, staring at my lighter skin. It is my hairy arms that seem to be most captivating for them.

'Monyet!' laughs one of the boys and the rest fall about laughing.

'Rifqi. What does Monyet mean?' I ask eagerly.

'Haha! It means monkey! They think you are hairy like a monkey.'

I pretend to chase after the boys as they go running off back to the grass thatched houses just behind our resting spot. In this moment, I realise how much I would love to start a family: a family of my own with Rifqi. My fantasy is broken by Amat's call to get back into the car. As we stroll towards the car, I take the opportunity to question Rifqi.

'What happened to Annisa's husband? Your mother seems quite upset by it.'

'Josef, her husband is Filipino. He has always worked away from home but he would always come back once a month, and give my sister money and spend time with the family,' explains Rifqi.

'And then…?' I push.

'Then, one day, he just didn't come home. Months passed and no sign.'

'What if he…' I pause.

'No. He calls my sister and talks on the phone to the children. He says he has no money to get back to Indonesia. I think he is a liar.' Rifqi looks angry. Angry for the pain inflicted on his sister. 'And this was just after Annisa was pregnant with Sari. I don't know how a man could abandon his own family,' Rifqi adds disappointedly.

Amat gives another call to us to hurry up and we continue our short ride to the ancient Buddhist site.

Exiting the car at the Borobudur temple, my excitement sores. This is my first time at the iconic Buddhist temple. I was not fortunate to have visited the sacred grounds during my last visit to Indonesia as my focus had been in Bali. We are greeted by countless local women offering us anything from sun umbrellas, water, wooden toys, mini stone replicas of the temples themselves and printed t-shirts. I feel like a celebrity negotiating the paparazzi as I struggle to push my way through the small crowd that insists on pursuing me.

'Cheap cheap, sir. Five dollars.'

'Have size, sir. What colour you like?'

'Help my family, Mr.'

Endless emotive phrases rouse the exact reaction they hope for – guilt. I reach for my wallet right on cue. Rifqi grabs my arm and smiles, 'Save your money, this is only the start. You will be broke by the time you get to the steps at this rate,' he smiles. 'Plus you need to bargain hard.'

With my wallet tucked safely away, I am able to take in the incredible scenery laid out in front of me. Words fail me.

Stood in the heart of the Kedu Valley, two hundred and fifty metres above sea-level, I am intimidated by the ancient temple complex before me. Awe and wonder scream out as I struggle to appreciate what my eyes are seeing. In the far distance, the mighty volcanic twins stand proud. Merapi continues to puff three thousand metres above sea level, justifying his name – Fire Mountain. His sister, Merbabu, watches in silence. Kilometres of lush, unspoilt greenage surround us from all angles. To the left, only a few indicators of modern life spoil the illusion – a small village of tin topped houses and a solitary mobile phone mast sits lonely in a field. Beyond this, modern life starts to encroach ready for battle with history. However, in all other directions, the land remains unaffected: virginal to the human touch. From here, I can appreciate the architectural miracle that has remained proudly since the 8th Century.

'How could they have possibly built such a structure in those days?' I ask.

'So you are impressed?' laughs Rifqi.

'*Impressed?* Rifqi, are you joking? I have never been so... speechless!'

The enormous smile on Rifqi's face reflects his sense of pride for his country.

As we move closer, I begin to understand the construction. Five concentric square terraces sit on a pyramidal base. At the top of the squares, lie a further three circular platforms with the most incredible monument, known in Buddhism as a stupa, completing the masterpiece. Rifqi's mother and sister remain at the bottom sheltered by the lanky palm trees that stand like centurions at the base of the temple, guarding the secrets that lie beyond. I imagine, his mother has toured this site a number of times during her lifetime. Amat pushes past me without apology and rushes on ahead, clearly unwilling to make small talk with us as we trundle up the first set of steep steps. The impact of uncontrolled tourism is evident. The steps are worn and in some areas crumbling, but this only adds to the historic character. Sadly, a few less respective visitors have felt the need to carve out their names on the expansive stones. The declarations of love do nothing to make up for the disrespect in my opinion. Each square terrace consists of endless corridors of history. Intricate visual representations illustrate the life of the Buddha. Acidic ash has attempted and failed to smoother the Buddhist teachings, and whilst twelve centuries have caused some erosion, the art remains. An enormous, living textbook designed to give enlightenment to Buddhists worldwide.

A group of giggling domestic tourists approach us, spoiling the silence.

'Photo, photo, please.' I assume they wish for me to take a picture of them but they grab me, and toss me into the centre of the group and pass the camera to Rifqi who is, of course, amused by his people's fascination with me. The sense of personal space is clearly absent in the group as they snuggle in too close.

'Satu... Dua... Tiga...' *Click.* The shutter closes.

'One more, Mr, please.'

I attempt to relax and enjoy the newfound attention, but as the older member of the group, whom I had assumed was the mother, grabs my arse as the camera clicks, I cannot contain my embarrassment which only spurs on more laughter. They stand staring at me, fascinated with my complexion and hairy arms. Rifqi pulls me out of their clutches, and thanks them in his local dialect before giggling and re-enacting the act of molestation. Amat appears right on cue. *Why does he always appear at the wrong bloody times!* He stands stone-faced, camouflaged by his surroundings. Silent. No words; no emotion. His silence unnerves me. I want him to tell us how much he despises us or scream and shout just to release the tension. Not knowing his feelings unnerves me most. I want Rifqi to see and feel the intimidation that I do. If Amat expressed his dislike for me in actual words, maybe then Rifqi could defend me and deal with my fiend. But no words come. The glare says enough. Rifqi grabs the top of my arm and we sidestep past Amat who continues to stare. I look back over my shoulder and see him mouth something but I am unable to decode.

30 minutes later, we make it to the top where we are greeted by countless stupas, each containing a statue of the Buddha who sits silently in prayer as if meditating. Some have suffered at the hands of Mother Nature. Centuries of natural and man-made disasters have had an impact. I stop. Silence. I

feel transported back to a time long forgotten as history, culture and spirituality embrace me.

An almighty bang followed by a series of low grumbles returns me quickly to reality. The ground beneath my feet sways from left to right causing me to stumble. A large stone from one stupa falls and Rifqi jumps on top of me, taking a blow to his back, yet sheltering me from harm. The motion is a new feeling to me but in less than five seconds it has passed.

'Was that an earthquake?' I yell.

'Sure was' groans Rifqi who is clearly hurt.

'My God. Your back. Are you okay? Are you injured? Shall I call someone?' I sound frantic.

'I am fine. Just taken my wind.' *How can I not giggle at that sentence?*

'You saved me, Rifqi,' I joke. 'My hero.;

'RIFQI!!' Amat flies around the corner, clearly in a panic about his brother's safety. *Jesus, he always picks his moments to appear.* His panic soon subsides as he discovers me lying beneath his brother. Clearly, not what he is thinking but who am I to explain I figure. His eyes haunt me. His body stiffens as if preparing to lash out but he simply turns and runs back down the steps below. We stand and look out across the valley. Merapi is angry. Clearly, the tectonic movement has stirred him from his slumber. Despite the distance, small overflows of fiery lava can be seen. I am petrified and Rifqi notices. We waste no further time gawping the growing rage of the louder of the twin mountains, and make our way back down the countless steps and through the endless corridors. Rifqi is cool and collected. He is in no apparent rush, stopping to admire some of the stone carvings he may have previously overlooked. His meandering slightly irritates me as my pulse is racing and I would rather sprint. I dare not go on ahead for fear of being lost in the maze of passageways. Reaching the bottom of the temple, I am relieved to find the rest of the family safe. Everyone tries to reassure me with a smile that everything is okay though I can't help but wonder if they are reassuring each other more. When we are back in the car, Amat definitely has the pedal to the floor. Rifqi attempts to play down the drama as thickening grey plumes of volcanic ash can be seen exiting the mouth of Merapi at an increasing rate. I am so grateful for the kilometres between us, giving us time to escape. Rifqi leans across Henry, who is now nestled into my shoulder, drifting in and out of sleep, and places his hand ever so gently on my lower arm.

'It happens all the time here. No need to worry. Every five years or so, Merapi wakes. I am sure *he* will calm down in an hour or so.'

Caught! Amat's eyes meet with mine in the rear view mirror. *Nothing escapes this man!* His eyes squint and the left corner of his upper lip rises like a rabid dog. I move my arm swiftly from beneath Rifqi which startles him. Annisa notices but smiles only.

'Sorry…' I silently mouth, nodding towards the psychopath in the front seat. Rifqi just grins and raises his eyebrows. I think he does not fully appreciate his brother's antagonism.

In just over an hour and after a short roadside stop to pick up some noodles, vegetables and grilled chicken, we arrive at Annisa's home situated not too far from the family compound. We take off our shoes at the entrance and I am welcomed into the house. Though much smaller than Rifqi's mother's home, I connect with many familiar items such as the large flat screen TV, microwave and Internet. I am thankful for the presence of air con. Curiosity tickles me – is there a "real" shower? I try to think of an excuse to wander but refrain when I see Amat sussing me out. Sari insists on showing me every possible toy and teddy in her collection. We are friends now lost in translation. She babbles away to me in words and sentences that have no meaning. My attempt at basic Indonesian phrases seems to confuse her more, though Henry is clearly amused by my efforts. I silently observe the interactions of the family. Despite the rumbles in the distance, no one seems phased. Smiles and giggles are plentiful, and even Amat seems relaxed.

'What time fly tomorrow?' Rifqi's mother asks with a little help from Rifqi.

'Midday,' I smile.

'Apa?' She seems confused.

'12 o'clock,' adds Rifqi who has now taken on the role of official translator. Amat smirks, clearly happy knowing that I will soon be out of the way and he will have his brother all to himself. I do not wish to leave Rifqi behind but with Ali's birthday tomorrow, I feel obliged to attend.

The family continue to talk for hours and Rifqi does his best to keep me in the loop, though the constant need to interpret for both sides tires him.

'Is it okay if we stay here tonight, Robbie?' I quickly calculate the number of rooms divided by the number of people and wonder about the logistics.

'No problem for me,' I reply.

'We can drive to my mum's place tomorrow to pick up the rest of your things before I take you to the airport. Some of your clothes are in that bag I brought today if you want to a shower. It's a proper shower!' Rifqi chuckles as he sees the relief on my face.

Lying in my miniature bed that Henry has kindly donated to me for the evening, I feel somewhat guilty knowing everyone else is squeezing in together. I long for Rifqi to join me. I miss his lips. His touch. I miss his smell. I wrap my arms around myself and try to replay the last time we made love. My crotch begins to swell so I quickly change my thoughts to Ali's birthday celebration in an attempt to suppress my arousal, as I slowly feel myself drifting off to sleep.

Chapter Fifteen

Plink... plink... PLINK, PLINK, PLINK. I wake suddenly to a gritty sound against my bedroom window. It is similar to the sound of hail though the frequency and intensity are increasing. The call to prayer confirms it is early morning but daylight appears AWOL. I peak through the blinds and see thick, rolling clouds of grey smoke filling the streets. A faint smell of sulphur seeps through the window as the gritty ash continues to throw itself against the glass. It is impossible to see beyond the perimeter wall of the house.

The door flies open and a less relaxed than usual Rifqi stands in the doorway.

'Hey, Robbie, you can't fly to Bali today. The volcano is at full eruption and the airport is closed. There are no flights into or out of Jogjakarta.'

Despite the concern about the volcano, I smirk, a part of me thankful that my stay with Rifqi will be prolonged, though missing Ali's birthday sucks.

I throw on a clean t-shirt and jeans, and step into the main living space where everyone is sitting fixated on the TV and sipping on some traditional Javanese tea. Sari and Henry are engrossed with their unusual painted snails that seem to be some kind of pet. They are totally disinterested in the drama being portrayed on the news channel and the reasons for the tension in the room. Henry occasionally glances at the TV but returns to his more entertaining snails.

'What's going on, Rifqi?' I ask, not really wanting to hear the answer.

'Last night, a number of explosions came from Merapi sending lava flowing towards the Gendol river.' I'm distracted by a nerve shattering image on the TV – a column of smoke can be seen rising to 5000 feet or more.

'People within 10km have been evacuated from the area but it is estimated that already 30 people have died.' I can feel my face drain of colour. 'Hey, it's okay. We are over 30km away. We are safe here if we stay indoors. But you are going to be stuck here for a few days.' Rifqi grins, indicating his pleasure at extending our time together, which brings a little colour back to my cheeks.

An unexpected clap of thunder makes Sari jump though Annisa is quick to comfort her. The room is eerily dark considering it is already 8 a.m. The lightening intensifies which only serves to exacerbate the situation. My limited geographical knowledge returns to me, recalling a distant memory of a geography lesson with Mr Manson. It is a common phenomenon for a volcano eruption to stimulate the start of a storm. I briefly consider why my brain would chose to remember this fact now.

Rifqi's mum passes a plate of food to me and gives a caring smile. She appears calm and collected. She asks Rifqi to translate, and explains that she has seen three past eruptions, two earthquakes and a tsunami in her coastal village when growing up. She knows the drill now. But little me is shit scared. This is totally outside of my comfort zone. I have no survival code for such events, having grown up in the UK where we are blessed with little threat from Mother Nature. The occasional flood or single day of heavy snowfall is as dramatic as things get. I try to remain calm as the smell of sulphur seems to intensify. I have no appetite but do not wish to offend my generous hosts. The smoked fish and mound of rice do nothing to stimulate my buds but I try. Annisa sits opposite me. She makes small balls of rice, and adds a slither of fish and alternates between feeding herself and Sari. I sense the absence of Amat's glare.

'Where is your brother, Rifqi?'

'He went to collect Rio from his friend's house where he stayed yesterday. Annisa wants to have him back here now with everything happening. He is probably just waiting until the main ash clouds pass over.'

A mobile phone beeps but no one reacts. Rifqi's phone starts to vibrate on the small coffee table, displaying Amat's name. Rifqi answers. Past the familiar 'hello', I am unable to understand the conversation, yet the anxiety in Rifqi's voice and the drastic change in his body language suggests a problem. Annisa springs to her feet and is crying. I wish I could comprehend the words being exchanged. I feel so isolated. Rifqi's mother comforts her daughter as Rifqi paces the room as if desperately seeking a solution. He hangs up and grabs his sister's hands. She sobs continuously. I bide my time waiting to ask for a translation. My heart pounds fearing the worst for Rio but I try to contain any emotion I feel rising. Rifqi grabs a set of keys and heads for the door. I need to know now.

'Rifqi. What's happened?' I feel selfish for interrupting but I cannot remain helpless and ignorant to the scenario unfolding before me,

'My brother tried to drive but... um... the ash cloud was so big and he could not see. He crashed and... how do you say? Um... knocked himself out? When he woke up, Rio was no longer in the car. Maybe he tried to get help or maybe he was afraid and ran away. I need to find them both now.' The cocktail of emotions inhibits Rifqi's ability to talk coherently in a language not his own.

'I'm coming with you. You cannot do this alone,' I reply without hesitation.

I was not prepared for what I see beyond the door. Daylight is being strangled, turning the streets to a murky grey. A fine layer of sand-sized ash lies upon the ground below and further flakes of sulphuric snow fall onto my naked arms, the volcanic heat still emitting. The street is eerily quiet except for the distant thunder rumbling against a backdrop of continuous lightning. Yet, no rain falls, only ash. Rifqi drives slowly down the small alley and out onto the main road. The traffic is intense. Thousands of cars carry frightened passengers from the hills surrounding Merapi and into the downtown area that *we* are now exiting. It feels somewhat strange to be moving towards an area being evacuated. My heart pounds. My throat dries. I am not prepared for such an event, unlike Rifqi who has lived in the shadows of these fiery mountains for three decades. But I sense his fear also, his anxiety for the fate of his young nephew. Soldiers and police stand sporadically on the roadside directing the traffic along the clogged roads on the opposite carriageway. The ash is thickening as we travel further from the sanctuary behind us. The windscreen wipers struggle to clear the black soot on the screen, making it near impossible to continue.

'Rifqi, it's not safe to continue driving. You can't see anything.'

'I have to find Rio. I can't leave him out here. He will be petrified. My brother is just at the end of this road.'

'Let's park and walk the rest of the way. We will be of no help if we also crash,' I plead.

Exiting the car, my lungs fill quickly with a rancid air making it difficult to breath. I am afraid. A light rain begins to fall turning the gritty particles into a slurry of slippery mud. Rifqi moves at a quicker pace. I feel disorientated, unable to see beyond my outstretched arms. I stop, desperately trying to take a deep inhale of breath.

'Rifqi? Rifqi!'

I hear his response but I cannot see him. I cannot see anything. The rain falls harder. I slip.

'Go on ahead to your brother. I can catch you up,' I shout to Rifqi.

I take shelter in the doorway of a deserted shop. The tiny whimpers of someone close by become apparent though I cannot sense their direction. I feel my way around the perimeter of the shop and sat huddled against the outer wall of a small outbuilding is a young lad. It is too difficult to be see beyond a few feet but the shadowy silhouette suggests it may be Rio. I call out his name. No response. Fear holds the tongue of this frightened youngster.

'Hang on, Rio. I am coming.' The words are not understood but I have to try to comfort him. A creaking sound increases in intensity. Looking up, I can barely see beyond my stretch but the blurry image still screams danger. The weight of the wet ash on the rooftop of the dilapidated building against which Rio now rests is too much and the structure is collapsing right above where he sits. With no time to calculate the risks, I lunge forward into an unclear space, and stretch out my arms and grab. I feel the heat of Rio's body and yank him backwards, stumbling and falling onto my back with Rio landing on my chest as the roof finally gives way and crashes at my feet, covering us both in thick black soot and scattered debris. I shield Rio's face and mouth, and press my lips tight to seal my mouth. Rio lay still on my chest, stunned by the drama. Relief paralyses me for a few minutes as I force myself not to consider what could have happened.

As we clamber to our feet, Rio recognises me and wraps his arms around me, squeezing tightly.

'Terima kasih Mas,' he whispers as I feel a tear or two drop onto my arms. I feel equally emotional yet so relieved, as we stagger out on to the street. The faint outline of two figures can be seen moving towards us. One appears to be supporting the weight of another. I call out Rifqi's name in the hope it is the brothers reunited. Rifqi shouts back and our voices guide us back to each other. Amat has a wound below his left eye and appears shaken. When he notices his nephew behind me, he falls to his knees. Clearly, the relief of not knowing the fate of his nephew was too much to contain. He shouts words of praise to Allah: his emotions running free. Rifqi helps him to his feet, and the two brothers grab their nephew and hug. Rio appears to explain what happened and my involvement, and Amat breaks away briefly to signal to me to join the circle. I am totally shocked by the gesture, yet jump for the opportunity to embrace a less hostile Amat.

'You save my family. You are a good man,' Amat cries. Rifqi squeezes my shoulder and whispers, 'Thank you.'

We take a slow walk down the street back to Rifqi's car. Rifqi supports Amat and Rio just keeps smiling at me. After an incredibly slow crawl back in traffic, we arrive at the house. The entire family is there to greet us. Tears and gestures of thanksgiving are plentiful. Rifqi's mother bows repeatedly to me when Amat explains my act of "heroism". Tears of relief wet her fragile face. The anguish of the last few hours has taken its toll. Annisa refuses to let go of her eldest. Rio speaks no words, shock most certainly taking her hold. I retreat to my room to allow the family some time to reunite. I ponder on the dangers I faced and my body begins to shake. I have surprised myself. Able to face a situation so unknown and so unfamiliar. Yet, my fear was so real. I feel so proud. All of my life I felt so weak at times. Always in the shadow of a more confident father followed by an even more confident Max. I was almost submissive. I have been ignored by others, stood unnoticed, moved through life without a real impact. But today I have stepped up. The hero of the hour. I have demonstrated that fear does not need to disable me but empower me. *Maybe this would have finally made your father proud.* Thoughts of Max and his infidelity that I so foolishly accepted because of fear try to taunt me again but I just laugh back at my memory. Whoever I was before is not the person I am today nor the person I will continue to be tomorrow. Rifqi has helped me to see that I can be whoever I want to be and achieve whatever I want to achieve. I am elated.

The door creaks open stirring me from my moment of self-appreciation.

'Thank you, Robbie. Thank you so much.' Amat stands before me. His persona so alien though so much more welcomed. *He is rather more attractive without the anger.*

'No need to thank me, Amat. I am just so happy we found you both safe. This has been a day I will not forget for a long time to come.' Amat gives a warm smile to me and steps out of the room.

Just as he exits, he turns back, 'Please join us for a family dinner next week. We have special guests and I would like you to be there too.' I am rather shocked but pleasantly moved by the kind gesture.

After a much needed (warm) shower and an apologetic birthday phone call to Ali, I join the others to sit down to watch the full scale of the past 48 hours unveil on the local news. I cannot understand the words but the pictures give enough meaning and the occasional translation by Rifqi tells me all I need to know. 150 people lost their lives in the neighbouring villages to Merapi, refusing to move out of their homes. Others died from collapsing buildings or car accidents from poor visibility. No one talks at this point. For a family familiar with the force of Mother Nature, this has been one encounter that will forever remain a little too close for comfort.

Chapter Sixteen

After a further five days of being grounded, I have finally received notification of my rescheduled flight for this coming Wednesday. That gives me just two more days with Rifqi and his family. Despite the drama of the eruption and the initial welcome, I have really enjoyed getting to know Rifqi's family. Even though I feel like I have overstayed my welcome, I am thrilled. 'What's the plan for today?' I ask Rifqi like an excited child on Christmas Eve. He seems somewhat distracted and his pacing suggests he is apprehensive about something.

'I thought I would take you to the Sultan's Palace nearby and then maybe some local street food? You must try it before you leave.'

'Will we be back in time for the family dinner this evening?' I ask.

'How do you know about that?' Rifqi snaps back. Realising the harshness of his response, he lowers his head.

'Amat invited me last week. Is it a problem?' I question, feeling slightly confused by Rifqi. He bites on his nails before responding.

'It's fine, but I think no need for you to join. I thought you may wish to go souvenir shopping.' Rifqi does not look at me once but passes me a mug of Javanese coffee and a selection of satay. Not my usual breakfast but nothing is "usual" anymore and that's what I am loving.

'Rifqi… why don't you sit down and relax. You seem a bit anxious. Is everything okay?' Rifqi joins me for breakfast but does not respond to my comment. He places his hand on mine which tells me he is grateful for my concern. I change the topic of conversation to divert him away from his thoughts.

'Is it safe to go outside now?' I ask.

'It's fine. The rain has washed most of the ash away. We just have to take a little more care that's all,' Rifqi responds.

The house is surprisingly quiet. Amat has taken Rifqi's mother back to her own home, and Annisa and the children are out shopping at a local market.

I lean in, and kiss Rifqi's forehead and simply grin.

'Why are you looking me like that?' he asks.

'Simply because I love you, Mr Permana.'

'And I love you, Robbie.' I tingle from top to toe and can't resist but lean in for another cheeky kiss, this time allowing the moment to linger. Rifqi appears to appreciate it, placing his incredibly soft palm on my cheek and gently forcing my lips apart with his tongue. Paralysed by his bravery, my eyes widen. His tongue explores my mouth as his breathing intensifies. Sat knees to knees, he opens his legs and pulls me closer to his body. I do not put up a fight. His kiss is deeper. I run my hands along the outside of his thighs, up along his abs and completing my journey on his chest. The sculpture never fails to impress me: the idol of any artist. He bites my bottom lip gently, initiating my shaft to swell which struggles to find the space to grow inside the confines of my slim fit jeans. Rifqi parts lips before planting them firmly on my neck just below my jaw line. It feels incredible. Waves of pleasure wash over me. It tickles yet it's electrifying. A delightful mixture of ecstasy and arousal. I feel his breath gently dance into my ear canal. Soft. Warm. Sensual.

'I want you to make love to me, Robbie.'

My head tells me to stop. *What if Annisa was to return? We are in someone else's home.* But I cannot stop. I want this. I *need* this. For over a week, I have had to sleep alone knowing this beautiful man is lying alone in another room. I have longed to smell his familiar scent. To kiss his plump lips and taste him. I cannot resist him. He pulls my t-shirt over my head, and immediately licks and teases my gorged nipples. The sensation curls my toes. Left to right and back to left. I pull at Rifqi's shirt, the central button flying off across the room, landing on the coffee table to the side. It does not disturb the moment. I slip my hand inside and massage his chest tenderly.

'That feels so good,' he exhales.

'Good. That's the plan. You are so beautiful, Rifqi.'

He blushes. His skin feels so soft. My hands are in a frenzy. Caressing, touching, grabbing. I cannot get enough of him. Rifqi stands. His crotch directly in front of me, the outline of his erect penis clearly visible. Clearly inviting me. Slowly, I tackle his belt with one hand as the other one gently strokes his bulge. One… two… three… four… I pop the buttons of his jeans. I know I am teasing – it is my intention. I have waited so long for this and I want to prolong each sensation. I look up at Rifqi, asking for permission. His smile gives the signal I need. Hands either side of his jeans, I pull them to the floor. His penis springs out and proudly stares at me. Wrapping my palm around it, I lick the head. The taste is better than I remember. The deeper I take him, the louder the groan. It excites me further so I pick up the pace. His balls hang low and I flick my tongue around them before circling them in my palm. My hand slips lower and teases the tight opening of his arse. With his throbbing shaft back in my mouth, I gently push my middle finger into the warmth of his passage. He flinches slightly. The tightness is incredible and drives me insane. I slide in deeper reaching the swelling that is his prostate. Small strokes massage the gland, sending sensual impulses throughout Rifqi's body causing his knees to buckle slightly.

'What is that you are doing? It… feels… so… amazing!' Each word is spoken in slow motion as if struggling to catch enough breath to exhale the sounds. Small droplets of salty fluid drop onto my tongue. I slide a second finger in. Rifqi bites on his lower lip, and closes his eyes, the subtle mixture of pain and pleasure causing him confusion. I slowly scissor my fingers, stretching him further. I want to be deep inside him. To feel the heat of him as we become one.

'I'm going to cum, Robbie, if you don't stop,' he moans.

'Well that won't do. I have plans for you, Mr Permana. I want to make love to you.'

'I want it too,' Rifqi replies eagerly. It is the green light I seek, and I waste no time in spinning him around and pulling my jeans to the floor. I feel firmer than usual. The excitement strengthening my erection. His musculature from behind is equally impressive. A beautiful V-shape, a small perked bottom and tight thighs stand before me. I place my right hand on the middle of Rifqi's back and push gently, forcing him to lean forward as I step in between his legs that have already parted. I can hear his breathing – slow and shallow.

'Hang on. We need some lube or I will hurt you.' The technicalities kill the moment slightly. I shuffle, pants around ankles to my temporary room and frantically fumble in my wash bag for the small bottle of lube I packed in the hope of some action. Returning to my lover, I unscrew the top wildly, and squeeze the warm silky liquid onto my sweaty fingers and around his rim. My middle finger slips in with ease followed quickly by a second – the stretch causing a sensual burn that seems to pleasure Rifqi further. Deeper I dive, tapping slightly on the prostate that is now gorged.

'Please. I can't wait any longer, Robbie. I need to feel you inside me. I want to cum when you are in me.' With the condom firmly in place, I rotate my hips to find the perfect alignment for entry. I push harder though Rifqi is too tight. Kicking his legs to further part them, I feel the head of my cock move forward. It feels warm and moist despite the latex that divides us.

'Oh my God. Slowly. It feels so good, Robbie.' The compliment turns me on and I push deeper. Our bodies now unite. My chest lays down on his back as I kiss the back of his neck. Rifqi turns his head slightly and our lips meet. His tongue flicks at mine as I push back my hips, slowly retracting and then re-entering. Each movement feels better than the last, the lubricant now easing the journey. I feel him wrapped around my shaft, squeezing and contracting. He reaches down on begins to massage himself. As he picks up the pace, I feel him tighten his grip on me forcing the climax out of me. Spurts of ecstasy exit me. The deeper, harder thrusts hit Rifqi's spot causing him to cum. White ribbons shoot across the tiled floor beneath. Beads of sweat fall from the hairs of my chest and onto Rifqi's back below. The beat of his heart amplifies through his back and into the cavity of my chest.

Chapter Seventeen

Jeans pulled up, we slump next to each other on the sofa, our naked torsos interlinked. Rifqi playfully fires a number of little kisses on my forehead, cheeks and lips.

'I think I need to shower,' I moan as I stand up and stretch my arms high above my chest. The door flies open and Amat steps in. I freeze. The scene looks like the aftermath of a Friday night at a gay sauna. Half-naked men lounging about, used condoms wrapped in tissues, bodily fluid spewed across the floor. I am mortified and Amat is clearly horrified. Rifqi busily tries to hide the evidence but it is too late. We are guilty and there will be no trial. Amat explodes in a scene similar to Merapi a few days earlier. Angry words bombarded at Rifqi. I do not wish to know the meaning. The tone tells me enough. Amat's eyes bulge and his skin reddens, visibly disgusted by the behaviour of his brother. He steps forward to Rifqi, wagging his finger in his face before pressing it directly in the centre of Rifqi's forehead. Amat spins on his heels towards me.

'You disgust me. You have ruined my brother's life with your gay things. You destroy my family's trust.'

'This has nothing to do with Robbie. I was gay before I met him,' Rifqi yells.

The revelation tips Amat over the edge. He yells something in Arabic, no doubt quoting some self-righteous religious phrase and slaps Rifqi hard across his left cheek. The sound resonates around the room. Rifqi does not retaliate but simply lowers himself to the seat below. His eyes look so sad, his heart so heavy. I cannot allow Amat to treat him this way and despite my better judgement, I lunge forward knocking him off balance, although he does not fall. He is not built like his brother but he draws great strength from his fury. Amat leans forward, places both his hands on his knees and drops his head. His breathing suggests he is calming.

'Amat,' I plead. 'I do respect your family but I love your brother and we cannot help how we feel for one another.'

My attempt to pacify fails. I notice his fists clench but my reactions are delayed. I take the full force of the blow to my lower lip, twisting my upper body, causing my knees to buckle and taking me down to the floor. A small pool of blood leaks from my broken lip, and a greater pool of regret and shame concentrates it. I cannot lift myself from the cold floor. My heart weighs too heavy in my chest. It hurts more than the physical pain of any punch. This has been the final showdown that I anticipated ever since my arrival. Amat has mentally taunted me for days. He has watched my every move, glared at every sign of possible affection I have displayed. I feel drained. I cannot fight him. Yet, it is Rifqi for whom I feel most sadness. Everything he has tried to protect others from I have now ruined. I have forced two brothers apart, and stomped upon the values and cultures of my hosts in order to satisfy my own selfish needs and desires. I lift my head slightly and see Rifqi's tears. The man I love so much is hurting and here I lay, helpless, soaked in my own guilt. *Did I lead him astray? Is Amat's anger justified – did I abuse the trust of his family?* For Rifqi, family is everything. It is central to his existence and he has allowed a lover of no more than a few weeks to potentially destroy it. I wonder if his tears are for himself. For the realisation that our destiny is not together. Or are they tears of hatred towards a brother who shows no support and instead encourages this farce of marrying a woman. Knowing how selfless Rifqi is, I believe, his tears are for the pain he feels he is inflicting on others. For failing to be the elder brother he should be and for failing to protect me from the clash of our two cultures. We are at arm's length, yet I have never felt so distant from him.

'You marry that girl, Rifqi, and you never see *him* again. Or I will tell the family and then you have nothing.' I note how Amat intentionally conveys his parting words in English – ensuring I am also clear on the meaning. The door slams as Amat makes a dramatic exit that rivals the entrance. I pull myself up to my knees, self-pity slowing me down.

'I am so sorry for my brother's behaviour. I am so ashamed, Robbie. I cannot imagine how you must feel about me and about my family,' he sobs as he half-heartedly mops the floor of an unusual blend of fluids: one the result of love, the other a result of anger.

Chapter Eighteen

The car crawls through the busy downtown streets. Endless motorcycles weave in between the cars looking to shave a few minutes from their journey. Horse and carriages wait at the roadside for eager tourists keen to revert to a more historical form of transport. The enormous stallions seem immune to the continuous revving of engines and over enthusiastic beeping. Locals litter the pavements, eating an array of street food, whilst a few tourists stop and stare at the enticing yet unknown dishes before them. The downtown is a hub of excitement which is far removed from the atmosphere in our car.

The silence deafens me. I feel so insecure. Rifqi has not spoken a single word since this morning's rather embarrassing and actually quite devastating incident with Amat. The possible repercussions twist and turn in my troubled mind like a threatening cyclone. No doubt, Rifqi's concerns are tenfold. The fear of losing his family is genuine and although I cannot directly relate to this emotion, I sense his anxiety. Amat forced him into a corner and the intensity of the encounter ripped the revelation from Rifqi's lips. Feelings of intense guilt wash over me. *If I had not met Rifqi, would he have continued to conceal his sexuality from his brother? Have I unintentionally diverted Rifqi from his true destiny?* I am so confused. My anger wages a war with my guilt. Both equally strong, both not giving in to the other. I have waited for so long to find a man like Rifqi and now this is going to be taken away from me by the selfishness of one brother. Do I allow my own needs to come between those of a family? My frustration soars.

I look across at Rifqi who pretends to focus on parking the car just outside the Royal Palace complex. Despite the morning melodrama, he insists on showing me more of his hometown before my flight back to Bali. I long to pick up on a point made earlier by Amat, though I know I will not like the answer. I resist. Placing my hand upon Rifqi's, I try to offer a reassuring smile. A half-hearted smile in return is my only reward as we step out from the car. Walking towards the palace entrance, Rifqi places his hand on my shoulder. The public sign of affection catches me off guard as he has always been so careful of this before.

'None of this is *your* fault, Robbie. Please don't ever question that. We come from two cultures: two worlds so distant in their thinking.'

'I feel so guilty,' I respond, lowering my head to avoid seeing Rifqi's reaction.

'Guilty because Amat caught us after sex?' he asks.

'No… well, that was embarrassing but I do not feel guilty for that. I feel guilty because of the anger I hold towards your family and culture for their attitudes towards gay love. I know I have no right to feel this way. They welcomed me into their home and this is how I show my gratitude. I have disrespected them which in turn means I have disrespected you. I feel ashamed even saying these words.' My voice begins to break when the realisation of hurting Rifqi hits me.

'It is Amat who should feel ashamed for the disrespect he has shown *you*. I invited you to my home and this is how we treat *you?*' Rifqi's tone changes as the sentence completes. His anger towards his brother is clearly evident.

'But I also try to understand my family and my culture despite not agreeing with it. I know it is hard for you to comprehend. Just leave my family to me to worry about. I feel as frustrated as you do but they are my family and I love them very much. Even Amat! I know it is a lot to ask of you but please forgive him. He is just so conditioned in religion and tradition.'

My throat swells with emotion and my eyes are washed in tears. The sincerity of this man moves me, yet frustration with his culture and religion tear at my heart.

'Of course, I forgive him,' I lie. 'Do you think he will tell the rest of your family? I could not live with myself if they turned their back on you because of me.' My head lowers in shame. Rifqi whispers my name but I ignore him. He repeats my name a little louder and more playful. I lift my head and our eyes connect.

'Amat has known for a long time that I have *these* feelings. There was a time when we once talked about everything and anything. We were like… soul mates… is that what you say?'

'Yes,' I smile.

'I never actually *told* him I was gay… well, not until today… but actually I think he just knew. I never discussed girls with him. He knew I liked fashion, disliked sport – the usual stereotypes I'm afraid and I think he assumed that I moved to Bali to "explore" that side of me.'

'So what changed? Why is he now so angry?' I question.

'As I mentioned before, Amat is unable to marry his girlfriend, Dewi, until I marry. It's our tradition.'

'I think there is more to it, Rifqi. It would not explain his anger towards gay people. Do you think he might also have feelings for…'

'No!' Rifqi interrupts with a surprisingly harsh tone. He pauses and then continues. 'Can we just forget it for now and concentrate on enjoying our last two days before you fly back?'

I feel like a scolded school child and so break away from his gaze. Rifqi senses my hurt and comes back at me a little softer. 'By the way, I hope to return to Bali myself next weekend.' Internally, this pleases me but externally, I remain sullen as we take a casual stroll towards the Sultan's official residence.

The palace complex lacks the splendour and riches traditionally associated with a Royal abode, yet I am no less enticed. There are no hordes of tourists blocking the main entrance, taking endless selfies. Just a steady stream of visitors, mainly locals, I assume. The residence is so understated that I wonder how many travel guides have mistakenly over-looked it. We step up to the black-ironed gates that are flagged by four large white columns and are greeted (in Indonesian) by two elderly gentlemen in traditional clothing. The man to the left is particularly weathered in appearance and I briefly wonder the tales each line of wisdom on his face could tell. Rifqi hands a small credit card sized ID card to the gentleman who immediately changes his persona and is frantically showing signs of respect to Rifqi, whilst also appearing to explain

something to his colleague. The man on the right now also appears to be bowing to Rifqi. *How terribly polite the local people are.* The somewhat younger gentleman of the two reaches out to shake Rifqi's hand and entombs it within his own.

'Is this the usual regular greeting? It's very impressive,' I comment. Rifqi looks a little embarrassed with the fuss and brushes it off.

'Oh... um... they knew my father...' He appears a little perplexed but I think no more of it and proceed into an expansive central courtyard. The centric and foremost pavilion is considerably larger, and more extravagant in design than the smaller stone gazebo buildings that surround it, each unique in design. Elaborate tiles combine beautifully to produce a masterpiece beneath our feet. Black painted columns stand proud in adjacent corners, each wearing gold patterns of intrinsic design. A large number of traditional instruments lie dormant, the reflected light from the metallic surfaces cascading across the ceramic floor.

'This is where the main ceremonies are held,' Rifqi proceeds to explain. 'It is used like a concert hall. These instruments are played during gamelan performances for the Sultan, a kind of traditional art with dancers. Hopefully, you may see them practising later,' Rifqi continues.

Large hollow, golden discs similar to gongs hang from beautifully decorated arches. The size of each one varies slightly and accounts for the differences in the sounds produced. Rows of metal drums or bonang sit side by side patiently waiting to be stimulated by the musician. To the left, a smaller white pavilion houses countless older local males who have taken up residency for the day, chit chatting about local news as the hours whistle on by. Each wears a batik sarong and matching head piece or udeng. A variety of plain coloured shirts are worn on top creating an array of colours. All are bare foot having left their simple sandals at the bottom of the steps as a mark of respect. Curious to know the topic of conversation, I wander over. The words have no meaning but the banter fascinates me no less. I long to be as relaxed in nature. To sit and talk with old friends, reminiscing about tales long past. I humour myself imagining them discussing the woes of married life, the joys of women they have entertained in their younger years or the state of the country's politics. One of the men catches my eye and gives a wide grin, revealing a mouth of few teeth. His cheeky grin is contagious as he joins his hand in prayer and bows towards me. I hear Rifqi call my name from the opposite side of the courtyard as he beckons me to join.

'Hey, the local people are so friendly. The men were all sitting around...'

'You should not wander off, Robbie,' Rifqi interrupts appearing a little irritated.

'Are you okay? Do you know those men?' I ask inquisitively.

'Um... they are just some old friends of my father. Come, let's go and explore the inside of the palace. Hopefully, it will be cooler indoors,' Rifqi answers, mopping the sweat from his brow. The humidity has curled the ends of his hair that now flops down on his forehead

The walkway towards the first room is lined with glass-fronted rooms that resemble enlarged display cabinets. Inside, a number of mannequins stand proud, providing a timeline of traditional clothing worn by different members of society through the centuries. The King's home doubles as a living museum and represents the pride of the Jogjakarta people. Entering the first room, the change in temperature provided by the stone walls is a welcomed relief. Beads of sweat chase each other down my sun-kissed back, forming a larger puddle at the base of my spine, which seeps through my t-shirt. The quick sip of water from my backpack eases the dehydration. Rifqi attempts to explain the history of transportation in Jogja as we move quick pace through the first exhibit. A number of horse-drawn carriages of various sizes and design stand grounded.

'These are the Royal carriages through the years,' explains Rifqi. I want to tell him that I have worked that out for myself but resist the temptation to sound sarcastic on account of his efforts. No further useful information is offered which makes me chuckle. The second room forms a small art gallery, though less grand in composition. Upon the bare brick walls sit a number of portraits of Sultans through the ages, as well as a small collection of photographs. I attempt to read the small descriptions below each frame but the English translation is either missing or limited in detail. The detail of the portraits fascinates me. I instantly make comparisons to the British Monarchy – comparing the clothing, the small clues in the pictures about the homes and lifestyle. The differences in culture and wealth are most notable.

'Let's go and watch the dance performance,' Rifqi says pulling on my arm.

'Hey, why the hurry, Mr? What happened to the laid back Asian pace of life?' I laugh.

Exiting the main room, my eye suddenly capture a familiar image to the right of the door. Above it reads an English translation, *Sultan 8.* I know I have seen this picture somewhere before but cannot recall. My memory lapse irritates me. I look closer at the photograph. A grandiose gentleman, two young boys and a little girl huddled around him. The formality of the image strikes me again. Instantly, my memory high-fives me. Although this image is much larger than the version I had previously encountered, there is no mistaking that this is indeed the same image I first met at Rifqi's home. Briefly, I assume that it is a mark of respect to hang a picture of the King in every household but it is Rifqi's behaviour that questions my logic. He fidgets with his hands behind me and avoids any eye contact. My mind starts to replay previous events: the incredible respect shown towards him by others; the large compound in which the family live; the attentive "staff" always on standby.

'*Rifqi*,' I ask gingerly. 'Is there something you are not telling me?'

He seems to know that he is cornered on this occasion. He takes a deep breath, drops his head and mumbles something so inaudible it makes me giggle. He makes a second attempt.

'My family…'

'*Yes!*' I interject like an over-excited child on Christmas morning. I am practically jumping for joy with what I anticipate Rifqi is about to reveal.

'My family are… well… my family are kind of… *Royal.* '

'*Eeeek.* ' Some sort of high pitched noise emits from me as I grab Rifqi, and jump up and down laughing uncontrollably. 'Are you serious? What do you mean *kind of*? Was your father a Sultan?'

'Noooo. My grandfather was Sultan 8. That is him in that picture with my father as a young boy. When he died, my father's elder brother became Sultan 9 and now this has passed to his son, my cousin,' explains Rifqi.

'Oh my God! Does that mean you are a prince?' The last word emitted at an octave higher than the others on account of the excitement of the revelation.

'I guess so. But it is not as grand as your Royal Family in England!'

'Yeah, yeah. But *you* are a PRINCE! *My* Prince, haha. I have actually slept with a real-life prince,' I jest.

'Well, that makes *you* a princess then.' Rifqi smiles. 'It is not a big thing honestly. It does not mean anything really. It's just ritual and tradition now. When Indonesia became one united Republican, the Royalty in each province was disbanded. However, Jogja and Solo were declared Special Administration Regions, and permitted to retain their Royal Family. The Sultan acts as Governor to the province. I have no role.'

'Oh, Rifqi, why are you always so modest? You are of Royal blood. It's fucking amazing!'

I am unable to focus on any of the other exhibitions at the palace, feeling that I should give a royal wave to passer-by or request to be carried and fanned on account of the heat. My daydream humours me as we exit through a rear gate. *Undercover to avoid the paparazzi, I suspect!*

We grab lunch at a local cafe providing time to talk. Rifqi remains silent, distracted almost and difficult to engage in conversation. I bob up and down in my seat; my head is full of so many questions. The young lad places a bowl of Javanese noodles in the centre of our table and two sets of chopsticks. He returns with two small side plates, interrupting as I prepare to commence my interrogation. I am unsure of where to start but without warning, a slice of anger appears on the table before me. She tempts me. It is not my intention to appear upset, yet, suddenly, I wonder why Rifqi has not revealed this significant information to me previously. *He told me he loved me.* How can you love someone and not share something so significant with them? So secretive. *Why is Rifqi so full of secrets?* So long, excitement. She has left the building. Stepping in for her now is paranoia and anger – welcome ladies, thanks for spoiling the fun. I prepare my first question. Return of waiter boy!

'For fuck's sake!' I exclaim louder than planned. Rifqi's eyes widen and his body tenses. The young lad looks terrified, and quickly delivers the plate of fried soya-bean and stir-fried vegetables to the table before scurrying off.

'Maaf Mas!' Rifqi shouts apologetically after him before scolding me with an intense glare.

'What the hell is wrong? One minute you are full of excitement about your little fairy tale and the next you act like some crazy tourist? You can't speak like that to people,' he states forcefully.

'Sorry. I just don't understand why you have never told me about your family before. You say you love me but you keep secrets from me,' I convey.

'I was trying to protect you, Robbie.'

'Protect me? Or protect you?' I retaliate.

'You!' protests Rifqi. The atmosphere is tense and neither us consider eating the food slowly wilting in front of us. Rifqi plays with the chopsticks, the tapping sound irritating my intolerant mind. The minutes seem to pass ever so slowly. I sense Rifqi looking at me but I want to remain annoyed and know that his puppy eyes will pull me back if I succumb to them.

'Well, both of us. I guess I was protecting both of us,' Rifqi explains.

I choose to still look out of the window, aware my behaviour is childish. *The tapping of those stick is driving me fucking crazy.* I grab at the chopsticks in Rifqi's hands, yanking them out and placing them on the table with slightly too much force. His eyes glare at me before he continues his justification.

'I was protecting all of us, I guess. Don't you understand now? Not only are our cultures so different but we are divided by religion and now this. Can you imagine the repercussions if people knew? The effect on my family? Everyone here knows my family.' Rifqi lowers his head and sighs deeply. I choose to hold my silence, despite the awkward atmosphere. I am not intentionally playing games but I am not sure of the best way to respond. The young waiter scurries passed me and I feel remorse for my previous outburst. The quick reflection changes my mood. I know I still need answers. Rifqi begins to eat as I throw out a question that seems to be logical.

'So why did you start this in the first place?' I ask, sounding more demanding than I had intended. 'You knew the problems it would cause and now I am in the middle of it.' My voice breaks on the last few words. Single tear drops fall reluctantly from each eye. I did not want to cry. I wanted to show that I am stronger than this. Rifqi appears embarrassed by my public display and passes me a napkin to indicate my need to toughen up quickly. He rubs his temples whilst closing his eyes. He is tense. *Is my behaviour stressing him out?* I quickly wipe my face, take two deep inhales of breath and relax myself. I sample the food before me though my appetite has moved on already. Rifqi opens his eyes and just looks at me. We exchange no words though so much emotion can be seen through these windows. Silently we continue to eat the lunch. I am numb to the flavours but the noodles satisfy my basic need.

'It was never my intention to start this, Robbie,' Rifqi starts. 'I told you, I have never been with a guy before. But that first night I met you, well, I just knew you were the person I was meant to be with. I fell for you, Robbie and I am still falling.' Rifqi covers his face with both palms before running them through his hair slowly but with agitation. I just listen patiently. Giving him the time to explain himself without interruption.

'I know it is wrong. I know it is complicated, yet I can't help how I feel about you,' Rifqi proclaims sweetly. He reaches out and grabs my hands. 'I love you so much, Robbie. I just don't know how to manage this.'

Water drowns his eyes and I perceive every emotion consuming him. I long to know how to solve his conflicts but reality tells me I am unable. This is *his* battle. The young girl to our left giggles as she delivers food to the couple sat next to her. She is clearly humoured by our forbidden public display of affection. My glare moves her on quickly. I consider the options for Rifqi and I – none thought through with proper consideration; only desperation fuels them.

'We can run away together. That's it! We will move to London where no one can dictate how we live our lives there.

What do you think?' I ask frantically, clearly not thinking rationally.

Rifqi looks away, biting on his bottom lip. I have never seen him so emotional. 'Not here, Robbie. Let's drive somewhere a little quieter. There is a beautiful ancient palace not far from here and unknown by many tourists. We can talk there.' Something inside of me knows that what he is about to say is going to break my heart.

Chapter Nineteen

The water cascades down the weathered terracotta walls, ending its journey in the turquoise pool below. The tranquil gardens of the Water Castle, or Tamansari Palace as it is traditionally known, provides the perfect space for reflection. A central courtyard filled with sapphire water is encompassed by high sandstone perimeter walls on all sides. Narrow pathways border the water and a single stone path crosses the mid-point of the courtyard. There are terracotta planting pots along the pathways and across the bridge. Identical shrubbery sits in each one. Crumbling steps lead down from the pathways into the still waters, indicating a historic bathing ritual in years gone by. The centric bridge essentially divides the tranquil aqua into two pools, each one housing a damaged fountain in its nucleus, suggesting a lack of maintenance.

My heart weighs heavy in my chest. I worry that Rifqi feels an imminent need to pull back from me. Frustration strangles me. If I needed to accept that he no longer loves me then I could deal with it. *Are you sure about that, Robbie?* But dealing with being separated from someone purely because of their family is incomprehensible. I know I cannot compete with blood. They have a lifetime of history together and we have all but a few weeks between us. I also know that his religion is so deeply entrenched in him. Realistically, I understand he will be at war with values imposed from a young age, and ingrained regularly by family and society.

I hold back for Rifqi to continue our conversation from lunch but he remains silent. I yearn for him to agree to move to London despite the naivety of it but right now, I would settle for even a negative response. I just want him to take control of this situation. My head and heart can no longer manage such affliction.

'Rifqi, how can this possibly continue?' I blurt out uncontrollably. *Why do my heart and mind never co-operate with each other!* Rifqi is struck by my sudden disclosure and looks confused but I give no opportunity for him to comment before I continue to babble.

'We have no future together. You are a God-damn prince, and I am the pauper and a gay one at that. This is impossible.' My voice completely shatters on the last word. It feels so much like a goodbye and one I am not ready for. Rifqi leans in closer, aware of a few prying eyes from local visitors and whispers, 'I am not letting you go, Robbie. I cannot. I do not know *how* this can continue but I certainly know that I want it to.'

Surprisingly, the beautiful words do nothing to morph my own feelings. Rifqi's naivety rivals my own and I am so afraid of once again being hurt. I resist looking at him for I know those eyes will mesmerise me, entering my soul so deep, and igniting the passion and love that burns so strong for him.

The sun's rays are intense, grilling the back of my neck. My lips feel so dry and I long for a moist kiss from Rifqi to hydrate me. Being with Rifqi means a lifetime of never being able to act on impulse. Always having to consider who is watching. Always storytelling about the true nature of our relationship and never really achieving our "Happy Ever After". And I want that so badly. I want my Hollywood Rom-Com moments. I want my kisses in the rain, my romantic dinners, surprise gifts and declarations of love in the most embarrassing of situations.

'Let's take a walk, Robbie,' Rifqi initiates.

Passing through one of the many courtyard archways, we enter the interior of the palace. The inner corridors and coves provide shelter from the Javanese heat. One elder offers to give us a guided tour of the historical site but we politely decline. Despite the fascinating history of the location, we are not here for academia but to save a forbidden kind of love. Our meander takes us into a fascinating space. Four stairways from four corners of the palace lead down to an underground space, most likely used for prayer. I am drawn to this space by the sun beams that dart from each diagonal to a central platform. I leave Rifqi and journey down the weathered steps to the focal point. Standing here solo, I feel like I could address an audience. I consider if things could have been different. If I could have declared my love for the man stood at the top of these steps without judgement and prejudice, I would tell the world that our love is not wrong, and that they have no right to arbitrate and to keep us apart. I want to be brave and fight for a love that has touched me like no other but Rifqi and I are no fools, and we both know there are so many differences between us. A million miles may not separate us in terms of geography but in culture and values, they most certainly do. The sun passes behind a cloud and the room darkens. The shade reflects my heavy soul. My time with Rifqi seems to be coming to an end. Unexpectedly, it is me who is taking a stand. *How much you have grown, Robbie.* I am sorry for breaking his heart but I will not allow mine to shatter once more. It is already too fragmented for that. I tell myself that in another lifetime we will again meet. In a world where our love is not appraised. Assertively, I stand at the foot of the steps and look up at my prince. He knows. He senses that I have packed my suitcases and am waiting to leave. The light magnifies his beauty. The outline of his torso and chiselled face reflect back.

'I'm sorry,' I mouth to him. Immediately, he throws his hands to his face. His sobs amplify around the room. Echoes of his pain ring in my ears and cut me deep. This is not what I want but I know someone has to act. Someone has to draw a close on a hopeless situation no matter how much it hurts.

The drive home is silent. Words will not fix this. Promises can't be made. My flight leaves tomorrow and so I shall save my goodbye for then. The thought of a family dinner with unknown visitors this evening fills me with dread but it is the least I can do as a thank you to my hospitable guests. As we stop at traffic lights, Rifqi sits mute, staring out of the side window. Nothing of interest captures his prolonged attention. The car behind beeps repeatedly when the light turns green but Rifqi is immune to the sound.

'Rifqi. The lights are green,' I say softly. He does not respond to me. It is the absence of his voice that unnerves me. I would settle for angry, emotional or indifferent. Yet, the iron curtain discloses nothing to me. *Does he think this is easy for me?*

'Are you looking forward to the dinner this evening,' I randomly ask in the hope of shaking Rifqi from his silence.

'There is no need for you to join, Robbie,' he replies dismissively. Clearly, the hurt is sinking deeper. At the second set of traffic lights, Rifqi fidgets in his seat and wrings his hands.

'Why don't you take some time to wander around the downtown before you fly back?' asks Rifqi. 'There are some great shops in Malioboro for souvenirs.'

'Do you think I want anything to remind me of this time, Rifqi?' I snap back. 'To stir my memory of the time when I had to let you go? Anyway, your family invited me this evening. It would be rude to disappear.' My sentence was unfairly harsh in delivery. I sense my barriers are on their way back up. Whenever I feel hurt coming my way, I get defensive. Mother taught me that one. No one can break a cold heart!

Chapter Twenty

The guests of honour arrive just past seven. Amat is weirdly friendly and accommodating, and Rifqi distant. I have no idea who the guests are. I presume extended family though I see no family resemblance. A young lady accompanies a couple as they enter into the main living space at Rifqi's mother's home. Both ladies wear headscarves indicating they are Muslim, so I refrain from shaking their hands as I know this is not permitted. *Of course, this must be Dewi, Amat's girlfriend.* She is a beautiful combination of east and west. Her modesty is clear. Her hair and flesh suitably covered, yet her fashion is apparently western inspired. Her face is porcelain. No need for make-up; this skin is innately perfect. Incredibly long eye lashes frame intensely black eyes that glisten as she smiles. I can most definitely appreciate what Amat is attracted to. Her nails are manicured and elaborate Mendhi patterns can be seen trailing from the cuffs of her dress that screams designer. *Amat has done well!*

The young lady is unsure of what to make of me but gives a friendly glance and smiles. Rifqi's mother explains something about me in their mother tongue, and everyone just simultaneously looks at me and smiles. Annisa and the children arrive. Rio is quick to greet me by respectfully raising the back of my hand to his face. Henry coyly stares at me, biting his bottom lip, indicating he is still a little shy in my presence I see Rifqi so much in his nephews and nieces, and briefly consider the kind of father he would be. Annisa impresses me with a few sentences of English followed by her characteristic giggle. She is ladened with trays of what look like satay to accompany the spread no doubt prepared by the staff. She remains fixated on the same spot, between the living room and kitchen holding the trays, and grinning until Rifqi plays the gentleman and takes the food from her, allowing her to take a seat alongside the visitors with whom she is quite chatty. Rifqi takes the food to the dining room. Her innocent, docile nature is endearing and the love between the two siblings so warming.

As everyone takes a seat in the dining room, Rifqi appears to intentionally sit away from me. The conversation proceeds in Indonesian and I am out of the loop. It sounds terribly formal and Rifqi is not translating as he normally would. I assume he is hurting and reluctant to overly talk with me. I try to imagine I am engaged and occasionally smile, nod or laugh when others do. What captivates me is that all of the conversation and questions seem to always be directed at Rifqi, and not Amat. On a number of occasions, I look over at Rifqi, a plea in my eyes to help me understand the event but never once does he look back. Amat, who sits diagonally to me, has not spoken, yet wears an unsettling and menacing grin whenever he catches my eye. I squint my eyes trying to read Amat's face when suddenly, everyone starts to clap and laugh. Rifqi's mother is crying though they appear to be tears of happiness. Amat smirks at me as he wanders towards me.

He leans in and whispers, 'I told you that you will not destroy my family and that you will never be with Rifqi.' He pretends to fill my glass so as not to stir unwelcome attention from others. Rifqi notices and stares intently, trying to decode the conversation that is too far from his seat to be heard.

'She is beautiful, right?' Amat continues.

'Who? Dewi?' I ask innocently.

'That is not Dewi,' Amat laughs. 'This is Nadia, Rifqi's girlfriend. Oh sorry. I mean Rifqi's fiancé now.' He can hardly contain his pleasure as he sticks his dagger in deep. His eyes indicate such pleasure and the grin haunts my soul. He laughs loudly and pats my shoulder as if we are close friends sharing a joke before returning to his seat, and raising his glass as if in a toast to me.

I look across at Rifqi who continues to sit there grinning a false smile that fools everyone else in the room except me. How could he let me walk in to this situation?

He did try to warn you off and send you out this evening.

Everyone simultaneously gets up from their chairs, and start exchanging signs of affection and I assume congratulations. Rifqi intentionally avoids eye contact with me. I withdraw towards my room closely followed by Amat who grabs at my arm as we move down into the corridor away from the view of the happy family.

'You did this intentionally. You wanted to hurt me so bad that I would walk away. Well, congratulations, Amat. I have already told your brother *this* is over. So I guess you and your homophobic values win. Congratulations.' Amat still smirks and I want to return the punch he inflicted on me earlier. 'Go back into the room, Amat, and take a close look at your brother and ask yourself if he looks happy to you? If you can live with knowing that your own happiness has sacrificed his own then good for you, you self-righteous prick!'

Yanking my arm from Amat's grip, I flee to my room and frantically pack my case. I refuse to remain in this situation for a minute longer. I will make my apologies to the family, and pretend I misread my flight itinerary and that I need to leave earlier than planned. One night in a hotel has to be better than staying here. Amat bursts into my room. Clearly, breaking my heart was not enough for him, this evil Prince needs to rip my heart out, throw it to the floor and crush it beneath his foot. My hatred for this man soars.

'Oh leaving already?' he taunts.

I take a deep breath. 'Please apologise to everyone and explain that I need to catch my flight earlier than expected. Tell Rifqi... um... it does not matter. You won't pass the message on anyway.'

I step out into the cool evening air with no plan of action and leave the compound. I cannot bring myself to say goodbye. I think of my mother and the strategies she uses to dealing with anything emotional, and do the same: total detachment until in the privacy of my own space.

'Wait, Robbie! Where are you going?' shouts Rifqi, running down the street after me. He looks as heartbroken as I feel. Deep down, I know this is not what he wants. I know he is only trying to do the right thing for his family. He grabs at both my arms but no words come from his lips. He has no words to share. He knows that Amat has told me. He is no fool.

'How could you let me witness that, Rifqi? If you loved me, you would never publicly stamp on my heart?' My words shame Rifqi. He drops his head and shakes it slowly. I do not want to prolong this moment. Both of us are hurting.

Despite my own pain, I love Rifqi enough to still want to protect him. I do not want to add to his torture. Placing two fingers beneath his chin, I tilt back his head.

'She is beautiful. I am sure you will be very happy together.' My words are spoken with a level of unintentional sarcasm. The conversation is hopeless. I turn quickly, jerking my arms from his grip and start to walk away.

'Please, Robbie. I want *you.*' Rifqi stumbles on the words but this does not stop them ringing out across the city, freezing me in my tracks, my back facing Rifqi as I take a moment to secretively smile at the gesture. It is the perfect movie moment. Flutters stimulate my heart, upping the tempo of the rhythm and butterflies dance about in my gut. But they are not real. It is my fantasy only. I refuse to allow myself to fall for such fleeting periods once more. I want ever-lasting. A love that defies any protestors. Rifqi cannot give me this. My smile retracts. I take a deep breath, drawing on all my strength and turn to look Rifqi straight in the face.

'Go back to your fiancé, Rifqi. You have made your choice. Now I am making mine.' I see the hurt on his face. The glisten of his eyes dries up, the trademark smile buried.

I cannot bear to prolong my stare, the pain ripping at my soul so I proceed to drag my case down the street. I never look back, yet, I hope he will come running, throwing my case to the floor and passionately kissing me as a declaration of his love for all to see. Instead, it's just me, my case and my once again broken self.

Chapter Twenty-One

The return flight to Denpasar is, thankfully, short so no time for overthinking after I shed a tear or two after take-off. Ali is fully prepared following my briefing on the latest saga over the phone, whilst waiting to board the flight. He will be on hand as usual to provide airport pick-up, accommodation and much needed distractions. No doubt he will have some wise words for me like, *Let's party!* I wish I could be more like Ali sometimes. Forever happy despite the challenges thrown at him. He too is trapped in the same hopeless situation with family expectations and imposed Islamic values. Maybe that is how he is able to be so empathetic. Yet, he remains positive about his life and deals with it silently.

Although heartbroken, I am looking forward to catching up with Ali. The only problem is that once again he is not on time as I enter arrivals. I'm not surprised and decide to make the most of the opportunity to browse the shops. My phone suddenly beeps alerting me to a text message from Ali.

Robbie. Sorry I am not at the airport. We have a bit of a situation here at the apartment. Explain when you arrive.

The text annoys me slightly as I just want to get back home as soon as possible but I know my annoyance is due to my own hurting and not directed at Ali. I imagine the definition of "situation" is a hot male whom Ali is snuggled up with in bed. I abandon my shopping, exit the airport and allow myself to be pounced on by the overly eager taxi touts.

The drive provides the time to catch up on some emails from back home and a distraction from obsessively thinking of Rifqi. My heart tries to force my mind to reflect back on my handsome prince but Mother's strategies prevent my fall into temptation. A string of emails from Kimberly sat among the endless spam mail make me chuckle. Her personality shines even in an email. The subject headings alone make me giggle: the drama of her tone having not heard from me in days. She feels abandoned and lonely after I have failed to return any texts or emails, and insults me for being the worst gay friend ever! We are close enough that I instinctively know that her accusations are all in jest and I promise myself I will catch up with her later. I had given her a snippet of information about Rifqi before I set off for Bali but left too much information out for her liking. The lack of details would surely be crucifying her. My brief smile soon fades with the realisation that there would be no need to share the missing data now that the affair had come and gone so quickly. The brevity of the relationship once again hits home. I start to beat myself for being so stupid. For again falling so quickly, so deeply.

The taxi comes to sudden stop outside of Ali's apartment. He comes rushing out to greet me, looking surprisingly perplexed.

'Oh, Robbie.' Ali says. 'I am so sorry. I didn't know what to do. He just turned up. I said you would not want to see him but he just said he would wait. I didn't even know he knew where we lived, and then I panicked and told him how you have been feeling recently, and then he seemed even more concerned and I tried to call you but you were flying...' Ali petered out as though he didn't know how to continue or what to say.

'Take a breath,' I interrupt. Despite wearing my apparently more sensible head, a part of me is delighted he has come. 'Don't worry, Ali. It's fine. Honestly.'

I bound up the stairs and into the cosy living space. 'Rifqi!' I screech with excitement.

The tall figure staring out of the window spins around. 'Who?'

'Max! What the fuck are you doing here?' I yell. Ali comes trotting in to the room, head down and refusing to make eye contact. I turn to Ali. 'Why the fuck have you allowed this prick into your home? I thought you were *my* friend?' I spin back around at Max who seems cool and un-phased by my outburst and anger.

'How the hell did you even know where I was?' I ask. Max looks over my shoulder at Ali, giving me all the information I need. I feel so let down by a friend I trusted so much. *Why would Ali do this? Was he jealous of my relationship with Rifqi?*

'Robbie,' says Ali. 'Just listen to what Max has to say.' Right now, I want to hurt Ali so badly for putting me back in this situation with Max, especially now when I am trying to deal with Rifqi. 'I am going to give you guys some space,' says Ali as he steps out of the room, closing the door behind him.

I stand staring at Max. Max stares back. He looks different. Maybe older, despite it only being weeks since we last saw each other. The sleazy image of him outstretched on the bed sparks a red mist to fall upon me again.

'What do you fucking want, Max? Whatever you have come to say, spare me. I'm not the same soft touch you manipulated for all those years. I have changed. I can take control of things for myself now.'

Max takes a deep breath. 'No one ever said you couldn't do that before, Robbie. You played that role.'

The comment arches my back and I punch my fist on the table, preparing for a full on defence. Max does not flinch at my actions. He looks lost. Emotionless. Something about Max troubles me. He is not his usual quick witted, arrogant self. He appears genuinely troubled rather than playing the role of a caveman who has come to drag me back to London.

'Sit down, Max,' I suggest more calmly as my rage takes to her bed for a while. 'I guess I know *why* you are here even if I don't actually want to hear it.'

'I don't think you do, Robbie.' Max lowers his head, his hands reaching up to cover his eyes as he starts to cry. At first, his cries are almost silent, except for the occasional whimpering but suddenly they transform to all out sobs. For a split second, I consider hugging him but my anger growls from within, reminding me of how Max made me feel in London. I say nothing but just sit opposite him and wait. A sinister part of me enjoys his pleas for attention. I hold the power now and I am not giving it back anytime soon. My heart beats against my chest, a reminder of the love we once shared.

'Robbie. I know what you saw in London, and I don't blame you for what you did and why you ran away. God, I was such a selfish prick.' The sobbing makes it difficult to understand each word but I decipher the general meaning. 'I accept things were not the way they should have been. I treated you badly and I deserved to lose you,' Max continues. *Pass me a fucking violin!*

'But it is not why I am here. The thing is...' He stops. Pauses. Rubs his forehead as if to release the tension and pauses again. I am bored of his show.

'YES!' I snap. My patience is now running thin.

Max gets to his feet and starts pacing again. He stands looking blankly out of the window I prepare myself for more of his lies and false promises but I feel I am immune to these now. *Sure about that, Robbie?* We wait in silence. I fiddle with Ali's health magazines on the table that fell out of alignment when I lashed out. I consider why Max is struggling to compose his lies which always seemed to flow so easily. Feeling totally fatigued by the drama of the build-up, I jump to my feet.

'I'll make a cup of tea whilst you get yourself together, Max.'

'Just like your mother,' snarls Max as I exit the room. The comment cuts deep, and I swivel back on my heels and re-enter the lounge.

'What the fuck did you just say? I never asked you to come here, Max. And why the hell would you bring my mother into this? I am nothing like her. If I was, I would still be in London whilst you continued to fuck every twink in sight. I left. This makes me nothing like my ever-suffering mother.' My voice is angry and my body language confrontational. I want to strangle this idiot right now.

Apparently, realising how much he has angered me, Max continues to sob, as he leans back against the wall and slides down to the tiled floor. His knees in the air and his head slumped forward, resting on his forearms that are crossed in front of him. I have never seen him so distressed and for the first time reconsider his motive for being in Bali. My anger begins to diffuse as I see this pathetic man before me. I remember the good times we shared together and my heart defrosts slightly. Despite my better judgement, I wander over to

117

Max and crouch down alongside him, placing my hand on the back of his exposed neck. The sign of affection spurs Max to a further breakdown. His crying seemingly makes it difficult for him to catch his breath.

'Max... look at me,' I whisper. 'This is not like you... tell me what's going on... *please.*'

Slowly, Max unfolds from his protective pose, and lifts his head and turns to face me. The sight is pitiful. His eyes are red and bloodshot. His face blotchy and his hair messy. The look is a far cry for the usually immaculate Max I last saw in London. *That* Max never had a hair out of a place, a dusty shoe, a less than perfect appearance. *That* Max never lost his shit like this. A sadistic part of my being enjoys seeing the roles reversed. For so long, I played the emotional wreck who needed Max to prop me up. I consider taking a selfie with Max to capture the moment.

Don't be so bitter, Robbie. You really will resemble your mother if you continue like this.

Max stares deep into my eyes. He is like Medusa. His look is transforming me from the inside out. I fight it but my defences seem weak in comparison. His breath brushes across my lips as he exhales, trying to compose himself now that the tears have passed. His head edges forwards as his stare continues to hold me hostage. Despite my resistance, my head is drawn towards his. I long to repel against the attraction but his force is too much. Our lips gently meet, and instantly I am weak and helpless. The taste is just how I remembered. Max's tongue parts my lips ever so gently and I close my eyes to savour the moment. Instantly, images of Rifqi taunt me. The recollection of Max's string of fuck buddies tease me. My eyes slam open, and I throw my head back and scramble to my feet.

'No! You are not doing this, Max. Not again. I am not falling for this shit. I won't let you wind me in like a helpless fish caught on your hook.' I feel so emotional. A mixture of guilt, hurt, confusion and pain. All caused by two men. One who looks broken on the floor before me and one who can't be with me.

'I need you to leave, Max.' I walk towards the door and open it, making it clear, I hope, to Max he needs to leave. 'I have found someone else. Someone who loves me for me and someone who shows me a kind of love you are incapable of,' I conclude.

Strangely, I talk of Rifqi as if we are still a couple. I chose to erase the recent breakup from my story. Max has no right to know the details.

'I HAVE HIV!' Max shouts. 'I have fucking HIV. That is why I am here. Not to win you back or to try to convince you to come back with me. Believe me, I want that but that is not my intention. I only came here to tell you. I could not bear to tell you via email. You have a right to know. You need to get yourself...'

I stop hearing the remainder of Max's sentence. My mind is now already racing. Too much information to process. Max has HIV and I know we had unprotected sex on many occasions before I finally opened my eyes to the realisation that I was not his only lover. *Oh my God, I need to be tested.* I try to rationalise the risk. We had not had sex in a long time.

'How long have you had this, Max?' My question sounds frantic and I realise I have not comforted him or told him how sorry I am. *You're sorry? This man has potentially infected you. What's wrong with you? You should kill the bastard right now.* I feel faint and return to sit on the sofa.

'The doctors are not sure but judging by the viral load in my body and thinking back to my sexual behaviour, I would say one year ago,' Max explains. He is calmer and more composed, totally oblivious to the implications of his disclosure.

'One year ago! One fucking year ago... we were still having sex then. I never suspected you were messing around then. What the hell?' I yell, before storming out of the lounge and into the kitchen space. My breathing intensifies and the reality of what Max has revealed strikes me hard. I grab at the sink counter and fight to stabilise my breathing. Fear and panic are taking hold. I lower my head and fight back my tears. I will not let this man break me again. The word HIV spins continuously around in my head. With each cycle around my mind, the volume intensifies. My knees weaken, and I feel light-headed as vomit rushes up from my gut and sprays into the sink before me. I begin to cry as I feel the touch of someone rubbing my lower back. I long for it to be Rifqi but instead, the man who has brought this to my door stands behind me. I wipe my lower lip with the back of my palm before spinning around and slapping Max with incredible force across his left cheek. The sound resonates around the tiny kitchen. Max grabs at his cheek. The shock on his face says it all. I regret my action but my anger strangles me.

'How could you do this to me? I loved you so much. You said you loved *me*, Max... if you loved me, you wouldn't have done this. Oh my God, Max, what have you done?' I am aware I am becoming slightly hysterical.

'I'm sorry,' Max shamefully whispers.

'You're *sorry*. Sorry? Oh well, that's okay then. If you are sorry, everything is okay. Do you know how many times I have heard that word from those lips? I am immune to it, Max. It no longer has meaning. Just like my feelings towards you.'

'Robbie. It does not mean you have contracted the virus. It's more complex than that.'

'Don't patronise me, you fucking prick. I know the risks, thank you,' I bark back angrily. 'The point is *you* put me at risk. Whether I have it or not, *you* risked my health through your own selfish actions.' My blood boils and I throw the nearest coffee mug against the kitchen wall, covering the floor with shards of china.

'And for that, I will be eternally sorry, Robbie. I can't justify it...'

'No, please don't,' I interrupt. 'I want you to leave, Max. Now!' My face reddens and I screech the final word through gritted teeth.

'Rob, I travelled from the other side of the world to tell you face to face. Please don't just throw me out,' Max pleads as he stretches out his arms as if to embrace me. I push his chest forcefully, causing him to take a few steps back.

'Should I be fucking grateful you came here? Do you know what? I actually thought you had come to tell me you had changed. That you wanted me back and would do anything to make it happen. But no... you only came to overload your guilt on me. Just go.' I feel exhausted. I have no fight left. I just long to be left alone.

The sound of the key turning in the entrance door can be heard as Ali gingerly creeps in. He looks sheepish. 'Is everything okay here?' he asks. 'Robbie, I am sorry. Max contacted me on email and asked for our address so he could forward something important to you. I didn't know he was going to show up here.' Ali looks really uncomfortable and I realise there is no blame to place on him. His intentions are only ever good.

'It's not your fault, Ali. Max was just leaving anyway.' Max says no words but his eyes plead for mercy. I turn my back on him and begin cleaning the sick that was sprayed in my reaction to Max's revelation. My bottom lip quivers as the emotions consume me. Every gram of bravery, courage and strength is needed to keep my back to Max as I know this will be the last time I see him. Each time, my heart reminds me of our previous love, my head slaps her hard. Behind me, I hear Ali and Max exchange pleasantries.

'I love you, Robbie. Always have, always will,' whispers Max from behind. Footsteps from behind become more distant and the main door closes. The sound signals for the onset of my breakdown. Tears of rage. Tears of fear. Tears of a love lost. Ali races in and hugs me so tightly. His heart is beating hard against my own torso. The love of our friendship radiates into my soul, calming me.

'Shhhhhh,' he whispers. 'I am so proud of you, Rob. You are a totally different guy to that one I first met in London.'

There in the stark white kitchen, Ali holds me close, reminding me of just how special a friend he really is.

Chapter Twenty-Two

For four days, three nights, I took to my bed. I had no other strategy to draw upon. I just wanted the world around me to disappear. Too much to consider – Rifqi, Max and the need to get a HIV test. The thought of being tested freaked me out. I knew I was putting off the inevitable but I could not find the strength to take myself to the clinic. So I did what I do best. I ignored it. Ali tried his best to motivate me but I managed to string him along with pretences about being unwell or stressed or just needing some space. I was too embarrassed to tell Ali that I stupidly have never had a HIV test before. Apart from hating needles, I have always been a little naive and assumed I would never contract the virus. I feel such a fool now. I knew Max was playing about and yet, I held on to this irresponsible notion. Ali was his usual supportive self – setting up the TV in the bedroom, providing a continuous supply of ice-cream, pizza, and chocolate as we spooned in bed watching back to back episodes of Sex and the City, just like when we were in Uni on the nights Max was out "entertaining". Ali has always had a talent for not pushing too much but at the same time, not allowing me to wallow for too long. In between episodes, we caught up on my short-lived adventure with Rifqi and in exchange, Ali updated me on his latest love interest – a Japanese businessman – married, of course.

Now, today is the day to rise from my pit of self-loathing and integrate back into society, and finally be brave enough to take the HIV test! *Well, that can wait until tomorrow – one thing at a time!* Kimberly has skyped me on several occasions and used hard love to motivate me. '*Stop wasting your life waiting around for some man to sweep you off your feet!*' she dictated. '*Toughen up, Mr and get on with your life!*' she continued. Luckily, I can take it from Kimberly. Her love for me is genuine and I know she only wants the best for me, even if her approach is sometimes a little tactless. Ali has lined up a job interview and so I have no further excuses to remain a recluse. Despite praying for the phone to ring or alert me to a text message from Rifqi, it has remained silent. In spite of the challenge, I decide to focus on the interview and becoming independent in Bali. Ali has been amazing but if I am to find a way of settling long term in Bali then I know we both need our own space. There is only so long two grown men can share a one-bedroom apartment. First step – a job, second step – finding my own place. I am not sure how well Ali will take the news. Despite the lack of space, he seems to welcome the company.

The interview is for a small web optimisation company based in downtown Bali. Most of the work involves dealing with clients in Jakarta and overseas within the impending ASEAN network. The sudden increase in foreign investment and overseas companies now relocating in South East Asia has made it necessary to recruit an English speaking web tech. Ali drops me off in the city centre and we agree to meet in a nearby coffee shop afterwards.

Just a short walk away, and I arrive at the address Ali has given me and step inside. The office is more of a room. Three technicians sit around the perimeter of the cramped space, surrounded by laptops, PCs and Macs. A solitary air con unit struggles to keep the temperature down. The limited storage has resulted in stock piles of papers and IT geek magazines cluttering up the place of business. The office is not a pleasant environment. There is an unusual odour to the room, a mixture of damp and cigarettes. The absence of any art work, ornaments, plants and colour indicates the lack of a creative touch.

'Selamat pagi,' I say to the room as no one makes eye contact with me when I open the door, attempting to use my increasing range of phrases. The three men immediately look up from their stations and exchange beaming grins.

'Ah, you speak Indonesian!' replies one, looking very impressed.

'Well, trying to learn,' I smile. 'I am Robbie. I have an interview with Pak Karma.'

Hearing his name, an older gentleman instantly appears from a small office space to the side. He is puffing away on a cigarette. He is round and short with a thick mop of black hair cut in a very seventies style – quite long despite the island growing on the crown. He has the most incredibly thick and bushy black moustache that fascinates me.

'Ah, Mr Robbie. Selamat datang. We are excite so much when Ali told us about you. You from UK, right? Please come come. This is Richie, Kenny and Anton.' My eyes are still fixated on Mr Karma's moustache. It appears to wriggle like a grub when he speaks. *Try to focus, Robbie, for God's sake!*

'Thank you so much, Pak Karma, for giving me the chance to interview with you. I really appreciate it.'

'Interview? You don't need interview. You have degree from UK. You have job!' Pak Karma breaks out into the most incredible laugh that comes from his belly with the occasional snort thrown in. He summons my new colleagues to make a space for me, and within an hour, I am all set up with my own desk, IT equipment and staff t-shirt ready for my first day tomorrow. As usual in Balinese culture, no one discusses salary or benefits. For now, I am just grateful to have a reason to get out of bed.

Following my rather bizarre non-interview, I bound over excitedly to the coffee shop. I am so thrilled to share my good news with Ali. He is sat waiting for me at the coffee bar. His little chicken legs swing on the bar stool on account of his height and hang from black sport shorts. The trendy Nike trainers indicate that work is going well. He immediately grins revealing his beautiful white teeth when he sees me strut in, as I am clearly displaying the persona of someone who has just been given a job.

'Oh I am so pleased for you,' he screeches.

'Because of you. Again! Thank you so much, Ali. I promise to repay you one day for all your kindness. Let me start by treating you to a coffee,' I snigger.

I meander over to the coffee counter, distracted by the mouth-watering display of cakes and chocolate treats. I refrain and order drinks only. *Time to get back to the gym, Robbie. No one likes a fat gay.* I place my order of two Americanos without even looking up. My eyes are still entranced on the sugary delights.

'Welcome to Bali, Mr May your life be filled with happiness,' says the young barrister as I spring back my head and catch sight of a rather dashing young man. He wears a plain white t-shirt that clings to his clearly exercised body. Large pectoral muscles push out and the tips of his nipples can be seen. His skin is flawless from top to toe. His black hair is incredibly thick and is brushed back with a side parting. A single diamond stud sits in his left ear lobe.

'Anything else?' he smiles.

'What? Um… yes… I mean, no. Thank you.' I am flustered. I try to regain some composure, telling myself he is probably still in his late teens. He giggles at my attempt to regain composure.

'Are you English, sir?' he asks exquisitely. I am flattered by his attention.

'Yes I am. How did you guess?' I ask, pushing for a compliment.

'I love the accent. So formal and polite. In a good way of course, Sir,' he responds with a cheeky wink before turning to the coffee machine behind, revealing the tightest butt I have ever seen. Black chinos snugly cover what I imagine to be a rather peachy bottom that hypnotises me.

'Robbie. ROBBIE!' calls Ali. I look over. 'Play it cool, for God's sake,' he mouths to me.

I perform an over-exaggerated stagger over to the table on account of being love struck, which results in both of us rolling about in laughter.

'My God he is *so* hot, Ali. Is this why you brought me here? Are you trying to distract me from Rifqi?'

'Two Americanos for two handsome men,' the barrister says as he squeezes between the two of us and places the coffee on the bar. An explosion of scent lingers as he steps back. A fruity mixture that makes my eyes roll. Ali and I burst into laughter once again. We are like a pair of pubescent girls when the college jocks walk through the school canteen.

'I heard he is also rather hung,' jests Ali as the barrister walks away and returns behind the counter.

'Oh shut up, Ali. You are such a storyteller.' A part of me contemplates the idea as I suggestively lick the coffee foam from my top lip as Mr Hottie catches my stare and gives another sexy wink.

'Time to focus, Ali. You are such a bad influence. Let's find me a place to live,' I state, as I lean over and grab the latest copy of the property brochure from the magazine rack to the side of our coffee bar.

'You don't need to find your own place. I am happy sharing,' says Ali.

'You have been overly generous already, Ali. And as much as I love you, I think we need our own beds. Your snoring and farting in bed are too much to bear,' I joke.

Another coffee and we are all set to start viewing properties. We have shortlisted three. All are within a ten-minute drive of Ali which was the compromise of me moving out. We both give a flirty wave to our coffee making hunk and are on our way, giggling as we fall out on to the street, bumping straight into one of the customers entering.

'Maaf Mas,' apologises Ali.

'No problem,' is the response. The accent clearly Indonesian but the response surprisingly spoken in English.

I jolt my head up from the listings page and stood in front of me is Rifqi. He looks equally shocked, though pleasantly surprised. I am mute. Ali's eyes are playing ping pong. They move repeatedly back and forth waiting for the first person to speak. He nudges me and his eyes widen indicating I should initiate.

'Um… Rifqi… um… how are you?' I stutter.

'RIFQI!!!' screeches Ali. 'This is Rifqi? Oh my God this is fate.' Ali's energy makes Rifqi laugh which eases the uncomfortable air between us.

'I am good, thank you, Robbie. I just returned to Bali this morning. I am sorry I have not called. I…'

'It's fine,' I intercept, though lying. 'It's probably for the best. Right?' I ask seeking his approval. Ali remains next to us fixated as if watching a soap opera. I catch his eyes and flick my head to the side indicating for him to give us some space. On the third attempt, he finally understands the gesture.

'You definitely played down how handsome he is. My God,' he squeals as he prances off to wait on a bench to the left of us.

'You look great, Robbie. Happy even,' smiles Rifqi. I find his comment almost insulting. Does he honestly think that less than a week after breaking my heart, I am actually happy? I chose not to bite. Deep down, I know it is only his attempt at being polite.

'I wouldn't exactly say happy, Rifqi. But I am trying and Ali has been great,' I reply. 'Oh and I just got a new job,' I boast, hoping to receive his approval.

I opt to leave out Max's drama and figure that whatever the outcome of my test result tomorrow, Rifqi was never in danger as we only ever practised safe sex.

'Congratulations, Robbie. I am so pleased for you. Why don't I take you out for dinner on the weekend to celebrate,' Rifqi suggests. It feels good to know he still cares but my eyes widen, suggesting my disapproval with the idea.

'As friends,' Rifqi quickly interjects. I further contemplate the idea as my eyes scan his entire body. The slim-fit cropped trousers look incredibly smart and exaggerate his height. The simple t-shirt adds a sense of youth to the outfit. I am weakened by his beauty. My defences shot down.

'Sure. Sounds great. Saturday 7pm at *Moments*?' I suggest, sounding surprisingly eager considering my reservations just moments ago.

'See you then. Enjoy your day.' As quick as he had arrived, he is gone. Ali comes pouncing over like a puppy, slapping my body, begging for details.

'Oh, Ali, what the hell am I doing? I told him *this* was over. Now I am going on a date again. Well, as friends anyway.'

'Relax, stress head. Just go with the flow and see what happens. That is one hot guy that you can't give up on easily. Correction. That is one hot prince you cannot give up on,' Ali laughs.

Chapter Twenty-Three

The tick ticking of the clock is slowly driving me insane as I sit waiting impatiently for my name to be called at the clinic. My stomach churns and I battle with the feeling that I am about to throw up. Ali had refused to allow me to delay the test any longer. He had me up out of bed, showered and packing a good hearty breakfast before chauffeuring me to the clinic entrance. We had sat outside for what seemed to be a long time before Ali finally persuaded me to exit the car. The clinic is a rather inconspicuous place. You would certainly not stumble across it. Funded by the Red Cross, it provides a discrete testing service, omitting the need to reveal your name and keeping the cost of the test to a minimum.

Each time the nurse enters the waiting room, I brace myself to hear my number called. It's almost like a game of bingo but without any fun. The other people waiting all try to avoid any eye contact. Maybe each one has a sordid tale to tell that explains their need for a discrete test. I find myself making judgements, forgetting that I am here for turning a blind eye to my partner's infidelity.

'Number 8. Number 8?' calls a tiny nurse from behind the wooden counter that hides her.

'That's me!' I exclaim with a nervous outburst. *It's not a lottery win for God's sake.*

The nurse shares a warm smile. 'Sir, please follow me. The doctor will see you now.' We move down a very narrow corridor before reaching a door on each side. The nurse slides open the door of treatment room 1 and we step in. A young doctor sits smiling behind a desk tapping away at his computer before looking up and pleasantly greeting me.

'Take a seat, sir. I just need to ask you some questions and then the nurse will take your blood,' the dashing doctor explains. I do not respond. I am too busy admiring the view on the opposite side of the table. Strangely, the very reason I am here seems to have slipped my mind.

'Sir, when did you last have sex?' the doctor commences.

I am not sure how to respond. 'Do you mean with the person who may have infected me or do you mean generally?'

'I mean the actual last time, sir,' he clarifies.

'Less than a week ago I guess.' I feel myself mysteriously blushing. I have no idea why since sex is such a natural activity but I feel like a teenager being questioned by my parents. My cheeks glow.

'Are you top or bottom, sir?' The doctor asks and without as much as a flinch in composure. He asks it as if asking do I take sugar in my tea. *Is this for his pleasure or for medical purposes?* Sensing my unease, the doctor proceeds, 'Statistically, there is more likelihood of contracting HIV if you are in the passive or bottom role, sir.'

'I like to mix it up,' I proudly state with a new found confidence and with that, the doctor gives a cheeky smirk. My gay-dar flashes uncontrollably but is suddenly switched off by the size of the needle the nurse is flicking, the tip of what appears to be an overly and unnecessarily large needle. Two minutes later and I back in the reception area for my thirty-minute wait for the results. The tiny dressing on the left arm is not as dramatic as I would have hoped but I still try to milk some sympathy from the staff.

Ordinarily in life, thirty minutes passes quickly. It's not long enough to watch a movie, listen to a music album, complete a gym routine and, if I am lucky, it's way shorter than any sex session I partake in. So how is it that these thirty minutes feel so long? I watch the seconds hand rotating around the clock face and convince myself it is moving slower than usual. After doing this for five minutes, I look for new entertainment. Next, I complete an imaginary redecoration of the clinic. I conclude that they need to add more colour, light and soft furnishings. *It's not a coffee shop.* Waves of nausea distract me from the project. My hands feel clammy and I am light headed. A single water dispenser stands alone in the corner so I walk over, take a paper cone and fill it with water. The sound makes me want to pee. Returning from the toilet, I check the clock once more. Ten minutes remaining. Fear takes a stronger hold of me. The wait is agonising. I contemplate the possibility of a positive result and the implications of this. The young lady to my right continues to stare at me. I think my neurotic behaviour is unnerving her. I consider for what reason she is visiting a sexual health clinic. I imagine her to be a high-end hooker with a case of crabs but that is only a futile attempt to lighten the mood in my gloomy mind.

'Excuse me,' I ask as I wander over to the counter to speak to one of the many nurses who appear busy doing nothing. 'How much longer do I have to wait? I am supposed to be back at work and it's only my first day.'

The first nurse whom I addressed looks at the second nurse, who looks at the third and so on. It is a like a domino effect, yet nobody gives me the desired answer. Finally, the first nurse plucks up the courage to say, 'Please sit down, sir. Five more minutes.'

My mind refuses to let my body rest. I stand up, wander, return to my sit and repeat the whole cycle again. The ticking gets louder in the room – it deafens me. I contemplate the conversation between myself and my parents where I reveal my condition, and they share their judgmental, prejudiced opinions in exchange. I think of Max and how I long to smash his face for putting me in this situation. I know that Ali has my back no matter what the outcome. I have already listened to hours of information sessions from him on the use of PrEP treatment and the success of this.

'Number 8?' calls the nurse softly.

My knees weaken and my heart picks up tempo as I begin to follow the nurse back down the corridor to the treatment room. I feel like I am walking to my execution, shackles around my ankles slowing me down. The nurse seems so far away. My vision blurs and my mouth dries suddenly. The sound of someone asking me if I am okay echoes in the distance. I am falling. Slowly.

The strong smell of eucalyptus fills my nostrils as I begin to open my eyes to the chaotic rambling around me. A single strobe light blinds me from above. I have no idea where I am or how I got here. Random faces bob in and out of my personal space. I try to sit up but someone pushes my chest down, 'Relax, sir. You have fainted.' Oh the shame of it. Why is it that I always have to bring a little bit of drama wherever I go? *Kimberley would be proud of this moment!*

Dr Interrogation is stood to the side smiling at me. He almost looks patronising but I prefer to assume he finds my display endearing.

'Okay, okay, I am fine now. Thank you. I didn't eat breakfast so my sugar level is probably low,' I suggest, eager to get my results and get out of the clinic quick time. I hear a snigger to the left.

'Oh you are a doctor now, are you? Self-diagnosis. Never a good idea, sir. People watch too many TV dramas and now everyone thinks they are a medic,' replies the doc.

'No, I just know my own body. Or maybe I am just freaked out waiting so long for these results,' I retort less patiently.

'I'm just joking with you, sir. You are fine. And your results are negative. Congratulations. But, sir…'

'Yes…'

'Play safe from now on.' I feel totally patronised though the cheeky wink at the end eases the moment. I drop my head back on the leather couch on which I lay and cover my face with my hands. I feel quite emotional. A strange mixture between relief but also guilt. Guilt that Max was not so lucky. *Max put you both in this situation. Goddammit!*

I struggle to shift the thoughts of Max out of my head as I take a fast pace walk to the office. I contemplate how different my feelings would be if the result had been positive. Would my anger have been fuelled by my own selfish worries then. I quickly text Ali the news, and desperately try to box the recent events with Max into the back of my mind for storage and later, disposal.

I slip into the office hoping my late arrival on day one has not been noted by Pak Karma. Richie notices my anxiety as I slide in behind my desk. 'Hey, relax, this is Bali. No one cares if you are late. This is the land of the free spirit remember,' he jokes. 'Anyway, I covered for you. I said you were stuck in the toilet on account of the spicy Indonesian food! Haha!' I was not sure I wanted to thank Richie for portraying this image to my new boss, but was grateful for the gesture. Richie seems like a great guy with impeccable English. He is an IT geek in every sense. There is nothing this guy does not know about IT, from technical hardware and software issues, to Internet and web design and optimisation. He is my IT guru. Kenny and Anton are more difficult to get to know as they are more hesitant to make small talk, though they smile continuously at me. I assume they lack the English skills or are wearier of foreigners.

'Where do you live, Robbie?' asks Richie. *Ah! One of the classic Balinese questions.*

I roll my eyes at Richie, 'Actually, I am sharing with my friend, Ali. But looking for my own place. We looked at many places yesterday but they are... um... not what I had in mind.'

'I have a few boarding rooms. They're quite simple, but clean, and you have your own toilet and shower,' replies Richie. I feel myself pout and look away, the thought of a cold bucket shower chilling me to my bones. Richie notices and laughs.

'It's an electric shower, don't worry. And the room is cheap. It's a good start for you. Why don't you take a look after work today?'

The rest of the day is a breeze. Life in Bali is so laid back in massive contrast with the London rat race. Pak Karma leaves us to do our thing whilst he sits smoking in his office. He occasionally comes out to make some small talk or grab a coffee. No one is stressed and we work at whatever pace is needed. *I think I am going to like this job.*

Four o'clock comes and Karma instructs us to go home. Richie offers to drive me to his home to show me the boarding room, and to meet his wife and children. Minus any traffic, the journey would be just five minutes, but we seem to crawl along for over twenty. I wonder why Richie does not choose to walk to work. The traffic is considerably worse since my first visit to the island. But even hours of traffic jams cannot rile the Balinese. They are so accepting of situations, and do not waste energy moaning and complaining about things that are out of their control. Ali seemed less impressed when I called to inform him about Richie's offer, insisting that I continue to stay at his apartment if I cannot find the right place. But my need to be independent is such a strong, personal desire right now. Of course, I could afford something more luxurious with the help of *Daddy's* money but I resist. This is about me standing on my own two feet. I have a job and hopefully soon, I will have my own place. I no longer need to stand depend on my father or Max. I want to come out of the shadows of others.

We pull into the driveway and are greeted by three tiny children – one girl in a little skirt and matching top, and two boys in shorts and flip flops only. They must all be under five. The two boys are very similar and I suspect they may be twins. They look so excited to see the man with the white face.

'They will think you are a celebrity,' jokes Richie. We step out of the car and the children come running over. The three of them share the same characteristic chubby cheeks and incredible eyes. The whites of their eyes have a blueish tinge to them, and the pupils are dense black and enlarged. The family exchange greetings before Richie introduces me to each one. The girl who is no more than two years old, is shy and hides behind her father's legs but the boys in comparison lack no confidence. Immediately, they surround me, touching the hairs on my arms and admiring my face with glee. I think my pointed nose captures their attention most.

'Richie, you have a beautiful family. You seem too young to have so many children,' I laugh.

'No, I am 25. That is not young.'

I reflect on my own pathetic life. Fast approaching 31 and not even a home to call my own. A string of hopeless relationships and a childish obsession with finding "real" love.

'Robbie? Are you okay?' asks Richie, clearly noticing my moment of self-loathing.

'Yes, sorry, Richie. I was just thinking of how lucky you are to have such a wonderful family. It's really amazing.'

'Well, we will have to find you a nice Balinese wife then!' replies Richie. It is at this moment that I realise that Richie has not even considered me to be gay. Of course, I hope it would not bother Richie if I told him I was gay but I decide that *this* is not the right time.

'You must stay for dinner,' insists Richie. 'You know how Indonesians love to host visitors and feed them!'

'I would love to,' I graciously accept.

Before we sit down for food in the main house, Richie shows me the boarding rooms. They are located at the rear of his property with a separate pathway that leads out to the main road. Each room has its own entrance door. There are five rooms in total sat side by side.

'Three are already rented. They have just been built so everything is very new and clean,' remarks Richie. He is beaming from ear to ear; proud of his achievement which will provide a nice additional income for his rapidly growing family. I step into the room and I am pleasantly surprised. The room is of course simple but the white tiled floor and freshly painted walls provide the perfect blank canvas. The all-important air con unit blasts a welcoming gust of cold air, quickly evaporating the tiny droplets of sweat running down my arms and back. A double bed, single wardrobe and cabinet frame the room. To the left, there is an en-suite. The shower is more of a wet room but delightful all the same. It is a far cry from my London Penthouse but it would be mine.

'I'll take it,' I eagerly shout.

'Really? But you have not asked how much?' laughs Richie.

'I was trying to be Balinese,' I jest. 'I thought we did not talk about money.'

We both break out in laughter at this. 'You are a funny guy, Mr Robbie.'

'Just call me Robbie.'

A wonderful spread is set up on the wooden terrace to the front of the main house. Avocado trees surround us and the sound of hidden island creatures coming out to play at dusk provides a musical ensemble. An alluring array of orange and red ribbons stream out from the sun that begins its decent to sleep. The slightly cooler air offers some relief from the tiring daylight heat. Richie's wife, Wayan, brings the final plate of cuisine heaven and joins us at the terrace. We all sit on the floor on a grass weaved rug. Richie's wife is very quiet but occasionally takes a sly glance at me. I assume her English is non-existent. The central large bowl consists of a classic Indonesian base food – nasi goreng or fried rice. The simple, yet incredibly delicious, dish is an integral part of any Indonesian meal. This national dish is surrounded by an array of beef and lamb satay, and fried chicken in banana-leaf. The mix of spices dances playfully in the air above, luring me in for a taste.

'Richie, I don't recognise this dish. What is it?' I ask.

'Ah, that would be Gado-Gado. One of our family favourites. It is vegetable salad with a peanut sauce. My wife has a secret recipe that makes this particularly special. You must try.' Richie looks across at his wife and gives her the biggest grin. He seems so proud of his family and rightfully so. The children behave impeccably. The youngest sits silently as her mother makes small balls of rice to feed her. The boys eagerly munch on endless sticks of satay, the peanut sauce smeared across their cheeky faces. Richie and his wife exchange words in their local island dialect. I fail to recognise any words but feel a little paranoid when they both suddenly turn to look at me.

'Robbie, my wife asks why you do not have a wife. I apologise for the directness of the question but I am sure you know how the Balinese like to gain a better understanding of their island companions.' I smile but inside I panic. I have not had to lie about my sexuality in the past. It is unfamiliar territory for me. I contemplate being honest knowing how accepting Balinese people are but I have just met these people. Maybe they are the exception to the rule? I choose to be creative with the truth instead.

'Well, I guess I have not been lucky in love so far. Not like you two.' I smile at my hosts and Richie provides the necessary translation. After a brief exchange between the couple, Richie returns to focus on me and continues,

'Ni Wayan says she has many friends looking for a husband and will help you find your special one.' It sounds incredibly business-like. I wonder if I should sign the contract now. I feel like I am being asked to select a puppy at the local pet store, not my future soul-mate. I am not offended by the suggestion. I understand the cultural differences and simply acknowledge the kind gesture with a smile and nod of my head, as I tuck in to my plate of gastronomy heaven.

'Richie, there is something I simply must ask you. I remember from my previous time in Bali that people are named according to the order in which they are born – just like your children,' I say, proud that I know the customs of the country that is rapidly becoming home.

Richie breaks into a huge grin. 'That is very true, Robbie. The first born in all families is always named Wayan, just like my wife and my first son. The second child is always named Made like my second boy who was born 2 minutes after his brother and the third is referred to Nyoman. This is my daughter's name. When we have our fourth child, I shall name him or her Ketut, which is the name used for the fourth born in a family.'

'It's incredible to think of how many people have the same name on the island. Doesn't it become confusing,' I ask slightly puzzled as I contemplate if the same system was applied in London. Imagine how many Johns, Richards, Marks and Williams there would be.

'Well, we also use a nickname sometimes. Hence that's why I am Richie. My real name is Made as I am the second born but my father loved Lionel Richie so he loved to call me this,' he laughs.

'Ah okay, now I understand. So I assume Kenny and Anton are not Balinese then? Or is Kenny named after Kenny Rogers?' I jest.

'Haha, very funny, Robbie. No Kenny is from Medan and Anton is from Jogjakarta. Naming your children with a set name according to their order of birth is a Balinese tradition only,' Richie concludes.

The boys entertain us with their fearless attempt at tree climbing for the following 30 minutes before Ni Wayan takes them inside to settle down for the night. Richie grabs some iced beers for us and we sit chatting about life in London versus life in Bali. Richie has an idyllic impression of what London life is like which I refrain from shattering. Who am I to take away his dream of a place he one day hopes to visit with his family?

'What are you running from, Robbie?' asks Richie quite unexpectedly. His questions throws me somewhat, and I cough and splutter on the mouthful of beer I have just swallowed.

'Why do you assume I am running from anything?' I reply, feeling slightly paranoid and sounding overly defensive.

'Your aura, Robbie. Us Balinese are incredibly sensitive to these things. I do not wish to cause you offence. But maybe I can help?' I ponder further on the question. I can't deny I am running but *what* exactly is it that I am running from? Max? My unloving, indifferent parents? The rat race of London? Suddenly, I feel like I have so much to run from.

'I prefer to think I am running towards something than *from* something. Hopefully, towards happiness,' I smile. Sadness stirs inside me, trying to lure me into a dark place but I resist her enticement.

'I understand, Mr Robbie. Well, you have come to the right place then. Bali... an island built on happiness,' Richie laughs as we raise our beer bottles to celebratory cheers in recognition of new beginnings.

Chapter Twenty-Four

I return to a silent apartment after Richie insisted on driving me home. A note on the fridge informs me that it's date night for Ali with his Bangkok lover. The apartment is eerie without the sound of Ali chatting away in the background. I stroll into the living room, keeping the lights switched off – the darkness a reflection of my mood. I am once again preoccupied with thoughts of Max. I replay the recent events with him in this very spot. Richie's question about running spins about in my mind.

I flip open my Mac and much to my delight, an email from Kimberly sits waiting patiently.

> *To the hottest gay in the world,*
> *Where the hell have you been? I have not heard from you in weeks. Okay, maybe not that long but it feels like it. Someone is getting a lot of action for sure!!*
> *Talking of action… Miss Jones has found herself a hot new lover. And this one comes in the form of a sexy Egyptian called Mustafa. A real life Egyptian! I feel like Cleopatra hahaha. And let's just say that the River Nile is not the only thing that is LONG. I couldn't walk for days. Now I understand why you insist on being a size queen. Hahaha!*
> *He wants me to meet his family but insists that I cover up my assets in the name of modesty. What a bloody cheeky! These are the best part of me I told him. Something about his family being Muslim so I am considering a makeover… well, a make under, I guess lol. Can you imagine me all covered up with no hair extensions and lashes removed??? Oh God, I'm having a palpitation at the thought. Maybe it's time for Mustafa*
> *to take a trip up the Nile haha.*

Oh I miss my gay best friend so much.

So when are you coming home? You must be done with Bali by now. You've had your mid-life crisis now, so come back and we can go shopping!

Love and squidgy hugs,
Reigning Fag Hag, Kim

Kimberly's email warms me from the inside out. I try to picture her dressed modestly, meeting the in-laws and I break out into hysterics. For sure, it is something she will not be able to maintain. That beauty queen is devoted to looking good. I reminisce about our years of friendship. She has always had my back and kept my spirits high in times of difficulty. I contemplate why I have not confided in her about Rifqi. I have always told Kimberly everything about my sad, pathetic life so why am I now holding back on this? Am I afraid she will try to talk some sense into me? I click REPLY and start to type. I do not know where to begin so I delete the first two words. Something prevents me from replying but I do not recognise it. Maybe this is the right time to break away? The foundation of our relationship is my drama, and I want to move on from this and maybe the only way to leave my drama behind is to leave Kimberly behind too. Bali is the new start I crave. I sit consumed by the silence around me. The light from the laptop providing the only illumination. I decide now is not the right time for making any more major decisions. Suddenly, I feel ashamed I would even contemplate walking about from Kimberly. I am so tired. I am obviously not thinking clearly.

All of a sudden, the door flies open and Ali stumbles in looking visibly upset. I have never seen him like this before. I think he is a little embarrassed to see me sat in the kitchen.

'Ali, what's wrong?'

'I am sorry, Robbie. I didn't know you'd be here. I don't want you to see me like this. It's nothing, honestly.' Ali exits the kitchen but then stops and steps back in. 'Robbie, why are you sat in silence and darkness?' Ali asks with a puzzled expression as he wipes his tears on the back of his hands.

'Just thinking, Ali,' I say. 'Come and sit down, and tell me what's happened.' I beckon for Ali to sit down as I turn the kettle on to make us both some tea. *Like mother, like son.*

'Anyway, it would make a change from you always listening to me droning on,' I add as I turn back to Ali, tea in hand. Ali forces a smile back. He sips on his tea but remains mute. I do not press for details. I know he will speak when he is ready. Despite the silence, I feel comforted by his presence. His little face looks so distressed and despite the blotchy complexion on account of his tears, I realise just how handsome he is. He has grown a little goatee beard in the last few days but he still looks like a teenager. For the first time, he seems so vulnerable.

'Do you ever get pissed off with how difficult it is being gay?' Ali asks with a noticeable level of anger in his voice. I do not answer but just look at him. I know there is more to come. 'I mean, why people can't just accept that some men love other men. What's the fucking problem?' Ali clenches his fist and strikes the table below, spilling some of the tea from our mugs. I give a half grin in return as I reflect on the similar situation with Rifqi.

'What's happened?' I question gently. Ali raises his hands to cover his face and begins to sob, at first with little sound but the pace soon picks up tempo. I get out of my chair and bear hug him from behind where he sits. My gesture seems to help Ali to release further emotion.

'Shhh, it's okay, Ali. Let it out,' I say. A part of me is enjoying being the comforter on this occasion, a welcomed relief from always being the centre of drama.

'I will never be happy... I mean, truly happy,' Ali sobs; his whole body feels so tense.

'Why do you say that?' I ask as I return to sit opposite him, holding his hands in my mine.

'Chai has ended things. He says he can't do this to his wife anymore.' Ali raises his head to look at me. His face is so red, his eyes reflecting his internal hurt.

'What happened to not getting attached, Ali? Love 'em and leave 'em is your motto.'

'I really liked this one,' he cries. 'I thought he was the one.' Ali drops his head to the table and the tears continue flowing. He bangs his head on the table repeatedly. I place my hand on the back of his head to comfort him. He calms. We just sit in silence for five minutes or so. Ali's revelation takes me by surprise. In all the time I have known him, he has never spoken

140

of any of his love interests in this way. I always figured he was immune to such emotions. Stupid of me really. Everyone with a heart runs the risk of falling. I understand it now. He was choosing not to fall because he knew he could never be with any of them due to his family and religion. I am intrigued to know what has changed with Ali.

'Ali, what is about Chai that made you fall?'

'Don't you get it, Robbie? Nothing has changed. It has all been an act. I way of keeping me immune to the feelings. I guess I have grown tired of pretending and I let my guard down.' He pauses as I try to process what he has told me. 'I'm such an idiot,' he yells as he clenches his fists and begins to lash out. 'Are we destined to be lonely old men, Robbie? Or forced into marriages we do not want?' Ali asks, not really requiring a response. He is just venting. His emotions continue to stream from his eyes and nostrils. It is a sorry sight and I feel sorry for his pain.

'And do you know what else?' Ali continues, his face once again reddening. 'Just minutes after Chai breaks my heart, my mother is calling asking when I will find a girl and marry,' Ali rants. 'God, sometimes I feel like I am suffocating.' The muscles in his neck tense as if preparing to release an almighty scream. He takes a few deep breaths and slowly the calmer, softer Ali I recognise returns. 'I wish I could return to London,' he states sounding almost defeated by the difficulties of his pretence in Bali.

Ali's words resonate with me. So much heartache imposed on us from others and their outdated views. My blood starts to boil as I see my friend in such pain. I kick back my chair and it falls to the floor with a crash. I smash both hands down on the table. The strike stings.

'Fuck this, Ali. It's not right!' I yell. Another victim forced into marrying a woman because that is what his society has decided is more appropriate. I pace about the room, so many frustrations eating away at me. So many things I want to scream out to the world. I look back at Ali. My outburst has not phased him; he is locked up in his own world right now. Three deep breaths and I remind myself this is about him. Lifting the chair from the floor, I sit back down opposite him and interlock my hands with his. He does not lift his head, his chin resting on his chest. The same pain joins us. Joined together with Ali, I feel stronger. My anger remains but a sudden realisation washes over me.

'Ali, no one has the right to dictate our lives. I'm not doing this anymore.' I stand to attention as if addressing parliament. 'I want Rifqi and I am going to get him, and I suggest you do the same with Chai. And fuck anyone who tells us we can't!' Ali looks at me blankly, clearly processing my idea. His facial muscles relax, his frown subsides and a flicker of light in his eyes returns. He pushes back his chair and stands proud with me. Determination fills us both.

'You are right, Robbie. I'm going to call Chai and tell him how I really feel.' Ali runs out of the kitchen, mobile in hand.

My inner strength impresses me and I feel empowered to take on anyone who dares to question my love for Rifqi. The thought of meeting him on the weekend fills me with excitement and of course, a dash of lust.

Chapter Twenty-Five

Ali – zero; The Wife – one point. Ali failed to win the heart of his Bangkok Boy. A romantic meal at a top restaurant that probably cost a week's salary and two tickets to London had Chai running scared. He fled from the restaurant at quick speed and has not even so much as replied to a single gesture from Ali. Ali's grand declaration of love was clearly wasted on Chai. I am pretty sure that Chai was only ever interested in the sex and when Ali showed emotion, Chai backed off. Tears and tantrums have occupied most of the past few days but nothing that some ice-cream, and back to back episodes of Will and Grace could not fix. Four days of trash TV "therapy", and Ali is back to work and his former bubbly self has somewhat returned. I cannot help thinking about our previous conversation when Ali revealed he has always been acting. How do I know if he really is okay or if this is yet another role he plays. One positive is that Ali seems to realise that this is how he could really feel if he found love with the right person and so has already started dating a new guy. I think he accepts this cannot be the case with a woman and is not prepared to sacrifice that in order to please his family only. It has given him the strength to confide in his parents about his sexuality this weekend. With me out of the way and now living at my new boarding room, Ali plans to invite his parents over for dinner before the big revelation. It fills me with hope that Rifqi too could find the strength to do the same.

Feeling a lot more positive about things with Rifqi and generally life in Bali, I decide that it is the right time to contact Kimberly via FaceTime. On the first attempt to call, there is no pick up. I persist and try a second time. A high pitched screeching blares into my ear piece.

'Kimberly darling, move the bloody laptop away from the TV,' I laugh. The camera of the laptop connects providing a fascinating view of Kimberly's cleavage as she attempts to relocate herself. I sit waiting patiently as she moves through various rooms before settling in her kitchen.

'Hiya, babe, look at you. You look Asian, you are so brown,' she giggles. I still cannot see her face so only her bosoms shake on screen with each laugh.

'Hun, I am not sure that is politically incorrect.'

'What?' she yells into the microphone. The connection clearly dropping. I had forgotten that Kimberly was technologically challenged.

'Kimberly love, lift the camera up to your face. I can only see your breasts and as nice as they are, I would like to see your face,' I chuckle.

'How do I do that?' she asks innocently.

Pling!

Clearly hitting the wrong button, we lose connection and so we start again.

'Sorry, babe,' Kimberly yells.

'Hun, you don't need to shout. I know I am thousands of miles away but it does not work like that,' I smile. 'Tilt the screen back so that the camera is pointing to that beautiful face,' I suggest. Slowly, the screen ascends up her body before finally capturing a rather scary looking Kimberly: face pack spread thickly and hair in rollers.

'Jesus Christ, tilt it back to your boobs. What the hell?' I jest.

'Shut up, you. This is what beautiful people have to do to look this good,' she replies, trying to smile though her facial moments are somewhat restricted by the thick clay she wears. For the next thirty minutes, I explain the events of my Balinese adventure – highs and lows.

'Oh, babe. I wish I could have been there for you. Why didn't you tell me? I knew something was wrong. I have a fifth sense.'

'Sixth sense, Kimberly,' I correct.

'What?' she mumbles barely audible on account of the mask not being completely dried. I struggle not to laugh.

'The correct saying is that you have a sixth sense,' I explain.

'Okay, whatever, I have one of those. And I can't believe that fucking idiot Max turned up. Where does he get off on hurting you?'

'I know. But I kicked him out. I actually took control, Hun. Your training has finally paid off,' I say proudly as I proceed to further explain the complications with Rifqi and his Royal background.

'Shut up! Are you messing with me?' Kimberly demands.

'Seriously. He is a prince. But it's not like in...'

'So that makes you a princess,' she interrupts before rolling about on camera with laughter. Endless jokes later and we finally get to the point of the conversation – how to seduce my prince. I am now equipped with some strategies, though some I decide to avoid as I am not sure how Rifqi would respond to talking dirty in public.

'And what about you, babe. Still dating Mustafa?' I ask.

'Do you think I would be making so much effort tonight if I was going to just throw a head scarf on? Mustafa is long gone. It's Christian now. From Chelmsford,' she explains. Her face cannot smile but her eyes glisten. Kimberly never takes herself too serious.

'Quite a difference from an Egyptian,' I laugh and before long, we are both in hysterics. A further thirty minutes later and we say our goodbyes so that I can prepare for my date.

Chapter Twenty-Six

It's date night and my levels of excitement are riding high. With my first salary in pocket, I am feeling sharp, independent for the first time and dressed to impress. The new attire is designed to allure my sexy prince. Applying the finishing touches to my hair, I peer at my reflection in the mirror. My confidence excites me. I do not recognise the guy staring back at me. The tanned skin certainly makes me look and feel healthier but I abandon the tight t-shirt on account of it being quite some time since I frequented a gym. I opt for a slim fit shirt and jeans, and I'm ready.

I resisted allowing Rifqi to pick me up from my boarding room. Partly because I was little embarrassed for him to see my single room but mainly because tonight I am in control. I will be calling the shots not him. I will refrain from being dazzled by his beauty and charm. I intentionally arrive at *Moments* a little late so as not to appear too keen. The classy wine bar and restaurant is a gem sat relatively unnoticed down a small side street off the main tourist area of Seminyak.

The doorman greets me with 'Selamat Datang Mas', and signals for me to proceed in. Wahyu is in the small lobby area busy on his phone and gives a nod of acknowledgement before continuing his conversation. It had been too much to expect Rifqi to come alone. Stepping inside the main dining area, I scan the area. Crushed purple velvet is certainly the main theme. The curtains and chairs complement one another in the perfect Parisian style. The black and white checked floor is a stark contrast but it works well. The lights are low making it difficult to see but to my right near the window, I spot him. He stands from his seat and beams a ray of light towards me. Instantly, my heart skips a beat or two. My knees wobble and a whoosh of adrenaline pumps through my arteries. I feel giddy and it's incredible; I feel like a teenager all over again. His eyes glisten as I practically skip towards him. He has really made an effort tonight. A crisp white shirt highlights the beautiful tone of his skin. A smart navy jacket and slim fit jeans finish the outfit to perfection. His hair is slightly longer than I remember. He looks happy and smiles. If this was the last time I saw Rifqi, I would forever remember that smile.

He pulls my chair out for me which surprises me considering the presence of a few other diners. His eyes never leave me. I am transfixed too. We have yet to exchange a single word. Our eyes and smiles communicate all that is needed for now. *God, I have missed him so much.* We place our orders, the silence finally broken.

'I've missed...'

'You look great...'

'Sorry you go first...'

'It's okay, after you...'

We continue to speak at the same time, one interrupting the other. The moment makes us both giggle. We return to smiling and gazing only – it is so much simpler. The waitress pours two glasses of red and slips away without us even noticing,

'You go first,' I suggest.

'I have really missed you. I feel lost without you. I never imagined I would or could feel this way about another person and certainly not with a man.' I savour the magic of Rifqi's words. So romantic, so Hollywood. 'I am so sorry for what happened in my hometown. Please forgive me?' His wide eyed puppy eyes make it impossible to resist and so I nod.

'Of course. I could never stay angry with you. I...' I decide to stop my sentence right there reminding myself of being in control tonight.

'I love you, Robbie. I always have and I always will.'

'I love you too, Rifqi.'

The young waiter overhears our declarations as he sets our main courses down on the table. He is unfazed and gives us both a cheeky grin before wishing us an enjoyable meal, and leaving us alone. The fusion food is divine: a unique combination of French cuisine with an indo twist. Three glasses of Merlot later and I am feeling a little light-headed. Rifqi continues to tease me as his legs continually brush passed mine, though I assume unintentionally. I long for him to place his hand on my arm, to send waves of electrifying excitement from my fingers to my toes but he maintains his usual controlled public composure.

'Shall we order dessert?' I suggest, trying to distract myself from my rising lustful thoughts.

'Let's skip. I have something more sweet for you back at my place,' replies Rifqi. He has *that* look in his eyes. The same one that morning we made love in Annisa's home. He is clearly horny and that excites me. Despite telling myself this would not end with sex, I cannot resist the need to see his naked torso and run my hands along those sculpted abs.

'You are naughty,' I say as I bite my lower lip intentionally trying to look seductive. *Kimberly taught me that one!*

'I could be, given a chance,' he giggles before regaining his composure and stiffening up his back. He flits between moments of being relaxed, and periods of his over-awareness and concern with others.

'Taxi!' I shout over my shoulder and we both break out into laughter. It feels so good to see him so happy. Just like the first time I met him.

Wahyu drives, and we playfully touch each other on the back seat, out of sight thanks to the discreet sliding screen between driver and passengers. Rifqi is hungry for love tonight. His breathing is shallow as he bites on the lobe of my left ear.

'Hmmmmm, you smell so good. I want to eat you,' Rifqi jokes.

'What about Wahyu?' I ask confused. 'Are you not worried he will tell your family?'

'Wahyu is fine. Don't worry about him. He works directly for me, not the family. We have known each other for a long time and his loyalties lie with me,' Rifqi explains.

'And does he know? I mean… does he know you are gay?' I question, stumbling on my words.

'Not exactly, but he is no fool. He is a man of few words but for sure, he is not stupid. He is a professional and so he focuses on what I pay him for.'

'And what exactly is that?' I push.

'To get me from place to place safely and on time, and adequately prepared. Now enough talking,' Rifqi says as he playfully nibbles on my neck.

'What's got into you tonight?' I laugh. Rifqi sits up puzzled.

'Into me? What does that mean?' he asks. The need to translate stumps me somewhat.

'It means, what's happened to you? What's made you so horny?'

'Youuuuuuuuuuu,' he moans as he dives in for a passionate kiss just as the car comes to a stop.

Wahyu opens the passenger suddenly and we quickly try to compose ourselves. My erection is screaming at me though remains contained inside my jeans that are now rather restricting. I pull out my shirt in an attempt to conceal my excitement from Wahyu. He just rolls his eyes but I see the slight hint of a smirk. He signals for me to step out.

'Where are we, Rifqi? Have you kidnapped me?' I playfully ask.

'You wish,' he retorts quickly.

'Guilty, sir. I cannot deny that.' I am aware now that my words are slightly slurred as the mixture of alcohol and hormones have taken their hold. Rifqi stumbles out of the car behind me.

'This is my palace,' he laughs. 'Okay, maybe not a palace but this is *my* home. Welcome.'

It may not be a palace in size but my jaw still visibly drops. The place is magnificent. We stand in a pebbled driveway with the most impressive glass cube before us. An electric door closes behind us, providing a screen between house and road. White-washed walls frame the remaining perimeter and to the left, water cascades down the wall ending in a sapphire pool, home to many Koi Carps. The entire front of the house folds back revealing an enormous open plan living space. Highly polished white tiles reflect the halogen lights above and provide a flawless contrast with the black granite worktops. State-of-the-art appliances fit integrally in the kitchen and an imposing flat screen sits on the grey wall in the living space. It is monochrome defined. Black leather sofas smothered in grey, white and black cushions are arranged in perfect formation. To

149

the rear of the property, a sizeable pool sits perfectly still. Rays of lights dance through the water.

'This is incredible, Rifqi.' I remember my own solitary room at the back of Richie's house and chuckle at the comparison. This is also a far cry from his traditional home in Jogjakarta. Rifqi dismisses Wahyu who is quickly followed out by a young maid I had not even noticed standing in the shadows.

'Fancy a swim?' Rifqi asks playfully as he throws down his jacket and unbuttons his shirt with haste.

'I don't have anything to wear, Rifqi.'

'Exactly!'

The sight of his tight torso, the light framing him perfectly is the only encouragement I need. Shirt thrown to the floor I yank down my jeans. Rifqi stands before me in all his glory. His manhood stands proud, providing the flattery I need. Slowly, he glides over and assists with undressing me. Kneeling before me, he lowers my trunks. My cock springs out and greets him eagerly. His tongue flickers over the pulsating head. Pre-cum seeps out in anticipation. I feel his warm breath as his mouth opens and edges forward. His lips close. The soft, moist lining surrounds my shaft. The sensation rocks through my body. Waves pulsate along my spine. I feel my balls tighten and jolt my hips back to pull out.

'Whoa, not so quick,' I plead. He stands to his feet, and places both hands on either side of my face and kisses me deeply. Passionately. I am unable to catch my breath. I taste my own cum on his tongue that circles my mouth and jousts with my tongue. Rifqi grabs my hand and leads me out into the pool area. He takes an impressive dive in, but mindful of my lack of co-ordination, I opt to slide in from the pool side. Rifqi stands in the centre of the pool like a proud peacock, his chest enlarged and on show. The water droplets on his skin glisten in the soft lighting from the perimeter. He raises both arms to his head and runs his fingers through his hair. I am convinced he is moving in slow motion. Every muscle of his upper body contracts and relaxes providing an impressive display of the male form. I slide through the tranquil water towards him. Lust has a firm grip on me. I want him right now. Rifqi drops below the surface before I reach him. I feel his mouth around my cock again. The sensation is unfamiliar but toe-curling. His mouth seals tightly around my shaft to aid his ability to remain submerged. My climax is close but I long to feel him inside of me. I want to prolong this moment for longer. I lower my body into the pool forcing him to remove his hold. He returns to the surface and our eyes meet. Nose to nose, we tread the water. Rifqi gently bites my neck. His lips feel incredible. I break away and swim to the edge of the pool. I feel him close behind me. From behind, his erect cock presses into my arse. Teasing. Tempting. His hands placed either side of my hips, he lifts me up; the weightlessness of my body in the water propels me up. I lean forward and grab onto the side of the pool. No warning given, his tongue is deep inside me. His hands spread my cheeks. The entrance pulsates in excitement with each flicker of his tongue. The circling motion is ecstatic. I feel his breath whistle in, relaxing me further. He slides a finger in. Deep. It feels so tight. I lift my head from the poolside and arch my back. My actions excite him, feeding his hunger for more. Deeper. Faster.

'You taste so good,' he moans.

'I need to feel you inside me, Rifqi.' His finger presses so deep inside hitting the spot. He gently massages my prostate that is gorged and ready to release. My legs spasm but he stops just at the right time.

'I think you are ready,' Rifqi moans in my left ear. Pulling back from me, he leaps from the pool in one athletic move.

'Ride me,' he asks and he lies on the pool edge, his cock pointing to the night sky above.

'We need protection, Rifqi.' My recent scare prompts my demands. He leans across to a small toiletry bag at the side of a solitary lounger.

'You planned this, Mr Permana! You little horny devil, you,' I giggle.

'No comment,' he replies with a cheeky grin. I take the condom from him and slide it along his shaft. Slowly. The head pulsates in my hand. I straddle him and slowly lower myself. My eyes hold his stare. I close my eyes and bite my bottom lip as he enters. The burn almost unbearable. Rifqi closes his eyes and takes a sudden inhale of breath before a slow moan emits. I rock my hips. Slowly. I squeeze the muscles tight, grasping his shaft which deepens his moans. Faster. The pace is quicker, the movements deeper. Holding myself steady, I grab at his chest. His nipples press into my palms. I lean forward, and kiss his lips as he lift his hips and pushes deeper still. The sharp pain eases quickly. We both push and release in tandem. His chest rises and falls, the skin flushed as his climax approaches. I hold my position and Rifqi takes the lead from below. His thighs slap against my cheeks with increasing speed and volume. I cannot catch my breath, and without warning, ribbons of white are released across his chest and abdomen. I feel my prostate press against his cock as he enters deeper and deeper. My body shudders with over-sensitivity. Rifqi cries out, and scrunches his eyes as his back arches and he pushes with all his strength. I feel his shaft swell, stretching me further as his body gives one final contraction. His body begins to relax and his breathing eases. I lift myself from him and lie alongside him. My head sits on his chest; the sound of his over-stimulated heart beats hard through his chest wall.

'That was incredible, Rifqi. YOU were incredible,' I declare.

'Sweet lips,' he jokes.

I run my hands across his chest. The muscles provide an incredible landscape.

'I am so happy you are back. I thought I had lost you,' I say as I snuggle in for a hug. I take a deep breath and sigh. 'The idea of you marrying that girl was killing me. I'm glad you have changed your mind,' I add.

Silence. Rifqi looks away and I feel his body tense beneath me. He does not speak but seems frozen.

'Rifqi?' I ask as I spring up to a sitting position. 'You *have* changed your mind, *right?*' I demand, a slight panic now rising up. I tell myself to keep calm but Rifqi's reluctance to answer only heightens my fears.

He lifts himself up on his elbows. 'Robbie… um… the thing is…'

'Yes,' I snap impatiently. I know what is coming but for some sadistic reason I need to hear him say the words.

'Oh my God, this is… um… sorry, Robbie… I thought you understood,' Rifqi stutters. His face is flushed. He sits up and although we are sat face to face, he avoids any eye contact.

'Understood *what* exactly, Rifqi?' I emphasise each word, the tone clearly pissed. My heart bangs at my chest wall as if desperate to escape. She cannot bear to be stamped on yet again. 'For fuck's sake, Rifqi! I thought you loved me?'

'I do. I do, I do love you, Rob,' Rifqi places both hands on my face and looks me deep in the eyes. My soul feels so exposed. 'You *know* I love you.'

My heart calms. The panic subsides.

'But...' Rifqi adds, shaking me back into a frenzy. 'I have to do this. I have to marry Nadia. I thought you understood.' Rifqi drops his head. The realisation of what he has done hopefully taunting him. This is the first time I have felt anything but love for Rifqi.

'Understood? Why the fuck would you think I understood. You bastard!' I yell. 'You used me for sex this evening.' I feel sick. My skin crawls at the idea of being a fool once more.

'I am so sorry. This was genuinely only meant to be dinner. I have missed you so much. I love you so much too. But the wedding is still going ahead.' Rifqi stands and wraps himself in one of the untouched white towels, and turns his back to me.

'I will marry on Tuesday. I fly back tomorrow.'

Chapter Twenty-Seven

A sharp pain cuts me deep. I feel used: a fool once more. Naked and pathetic, I push past Rifqi and hurry into the lounge, and dress hastily as I fight back the tears. I cannot escape quickly enough and I cannot bear to look at *him* right now.

'Wait,' Rifqi calls out as he steps in to the lounge, throwing his arms about. 'What choice do I really have?' Rifqi yells. His face reddens, the frustration of his situation apparently too much. He picks up his t-shirt and throws it across the room in a rage, yelling, 'I have NO choice.'

'You have a choice, Rifqi,' I reply very matter of fact as I slip on my shoes, aware the fumbling with the laces is not helping me exit as rapidly as planned. 'We *always* have a choice. But clearly, you do not chose me,' I begin to blub. My pathetic former self is returning for an encore: snotty nose, red eyes and with plenty of drama. I look across at Rifqi. Sad and pathetic I stand there rejected. *What a loser!* I see something in Rifqi's eyes as he slumps onto the sofa. Is it pity? Guilt or empathy?

'I choose you, I choose YOU!' Rifqi yells, pulling at his hair.

'Then don't go ahead with this wedding farce,' I plead.

There is a long pause. Neither of us speak. Neither of us move. The abeyance gives us breathing space to just stop and think logically instead of emotionally.

Rifqi scrapes back his wet hair from his forehead. 'But how can we be together? You will always have my heart, Robbie. But it has to be this way.' Rifqi throws his head back against the sofa repeatedly and thumps his fist on the arm rest. At this point, I realise this is not what he *really* wants. I see the hopelessness of the situation for him. But I see he loves me too and I realise it is still worth fighting for. *He* is worth fighting for. I race across to where he sits and kneel before him, placing both hands on his thighs.

'Rifqi,' I whine. 'Please do not do this to us,' I beg as I drop my head into his lap.

A tear drops on to the back of my neck. I lift my head slowly. My eyes locked on Rifqi who is now locked on me. Minutes pass, each one of us desperately searching our hearts and souls for a solution to an impossible problem.

'Run away with me!' I throw out randomly. I jump to my feet and straddle Rifqi, clasping his face. Excitement oozes from me: logic clearly not operating. 'We can go anywhere! As long as I am with you, I do not care where it is,' I babble. Rifqi does not respond. Silence swoops around the room. The sounds of the garden insects heightened. My heart sinks, my body slumps. Time to prepare for rejection. Rifqi frowns. I see the veins of his temples protruding. His eyes dart in different directions. And then it comes. That amazing, breath-taking, healing smile that only Rifqi can share. He is beaming.

'You are right, Robbie. Let's do this,' he says excitedly before throwing his arms around me and holding me so tight. It feels incredible. So safe. So secure.

'Are you sure?' I ask doubtfully. I am too scared to allow myself to believe this may really happen.

'Never been more certain,' Rifqi replies. 'Meet me Tuesday at Denpasar Airport. I will have Wahyu take care of everything and message you tomorrow.'

'Isn't that the day of the wedding? Won't you be in Jogjakarta?' I ask confused.

'I have to fly back to Jogjakarta to gather my things and I really think I should try to explain to Nadia,' replies Rifqi appearing somewhat apprehensive.

'Will you tell her the truth?' I question.

'I think she actually knows. I feel she knows this is not the right relationship for her but is equally being encouraged into this.'

I understand the anxieties Rifqi faces and long to be able to take them from him. All I can do is hold him tight and reassure him I am there for him no matter what.

155

The evening drama tires us both, though the excitement keeps us awake as we spoon on the bed. For hours, we just lay there, holding each other close, talking about our plans, hopes and dreams. Rifqi turns to face me, kisses me soothingly on my forehead and sniffs the nave of my neck. The light breeze of his breath tickles and makes me chuckle. Rifqi pulls me in closer. Our chests connected. Our hearts beat synchronised. My mind tells me to proceed with caution. Just hours ago, this man was confirming his marriage. My heart tells me to be compassionate. He was only considering marriage out of desperation and social pressure. Once he was given an alternative choice, he choose me. We snuggle up and close our eyes, and try to get some much needed rest. Excitement overpowers my exhaustion.

'Where will we go exactly, Rifqi?' I ask. Rifqi slowly opens his left eye and grins.

'Wherever you want, Robbie. Thailand, Vietnam, London or Rome. They are all there waiting for us,' he replies, as he turns on to his back beaming. I lay my head on his chest, and at that moment, I feel complete and finally at peace. My prince has come and this is my happy ending. *See those movies really do happen in real life also!*

'But what will we do for work, Rifqi?' I question, lifting my head from his chest.

'Robbie! Will you just relax. All these things will fall into place. I have money and I have contacts. Now shhhh!' Rifqi presses his index on my lips to signal my silence and then pushes my head down on his chest. His dominating gesture impresses me. Strong and protective. Eventually, I feel myself drifting off to sleep in what I hope will be my most peaceful sleep I have had in a long while.

Chapter Twenty-Eight

The following morning, Rifqi drops me at Ali's apartment. I do not want to return to my boarding room until I have talked with Ali. Although I do not yet know the exact details, I owe it to him to explain that Rifqi and I plan to leave Bali. He has been kind enough to let me stay with him and set me up with a job.

'Ali? Ali, are you here?' I call as I step into the kitchen space where I am confronted by a bare-chested, young Asian guy. I fight the temptation to admire his physique and instead ask where Ali is.

'I'm here, Robbie,' says Ali as he too joins in the kitchen in nothing more than a towel.

'Well, I would ask what is going on here,' I giggle. 'Though I am pretty sure I can work it out. You must be Chai, right?'

'That is me,' the young man replies as he gives me the characteristic Thai Wai greeting.

Slightly turning my back to Chai, I mouth to Ali, 'So he left his wife for you?' My eyes widen with each word spoken. Ali smirks before grinning from ear to ear and pretending to be coy. 'I am happy for you, Ali.'

'Chai, I am just going to have a quick chat with Robbie whilst I get dressed. Then I am all yours,' Ali explains to Chai, before leaning in and kissing his cheek.

Ali and I move to his bedroom. Clothes are strewn everywhere and the lamp has toppled off the bedside table. 'Gosh, you two are energetic,' I joke. Ali surprisingly blushes. I know how much he likes Chai because normally he would feed me every detail but this one he keeps to himself. I feel the need to act like the big brother and warn him about the complications of the relationship but seeing how happy he is, I cannot do it. I

157

just have to hope this is his happy ending too. Ali dresses in front of me. His skin is flawless: so exotic and enticing. The image distracts me slightly from attempting to explain my plan with Rifqi. Ali just nods and gives the occasional smile as I ramble away. I feel the need to elaborate on the details though realise I do not even know them myself. The vagueness of it all excites me. I feel so elated and I don't want anyone to knock me down. So I keep talking to prevent Ali from speaking in case he does not approve.

'Can I speak now?' Ali laughs as he pulls up his briefs, giving me a cheeky glimpse of his perked bottom. 'God, you can sure ramble, Mr Sparks. Do you think I was going to judge or try to discourage you?'

'I guess so. I admit I doubt it myself sometimes even though I know it is what I want,' I reply. Ali turns around to look at me. His torso is so lean. He walks over to me and holds both my hands.

'Robbie. I love you so much. I have loved you being here and yeah, I guess, selfishly, I hoped your life would be here in Bali. But, like you, I am a hopeless romantic and who am I to try to compete with a hot prince like Rifqi?' Ali laughs before giving me a little peck on the cheek. We both sit down on the edge of the bed and just smile at each other. I feel so content when in Ali's presence and the thought of giving up a life in Bali fills me with some apprehension.

'So where are you both heading?' Ali asks attentively as he throws on a white t-shirt, his hair messy and tousled.

I push back his hair as I answer, 'Um… not sure.' Ali's eyes widen. 'Don't look like that, Ali!' I retort before he even has chance to comment.

'Hey, I was about to say *how* exciting. Relax yourself. I am not going to judge you, Robbie. You deserve this, and I sense Rifqi has a good soul and will take care of you.' Ali places his hand on my thigh and gives it a friendly squeeze.

'Okay, so the location is a mystery… do you at least know when you will go?' Ali continues.

'Tuesday,' I reply grinning. The imminence of it so real.

'Then tonight we must party and give you a proper Balinese goodbye.' Ali throws his arms around me.

'Tonight, I need to go back to the boarding house and pack. Let's spend my last evening together. Is it okay if I stay at your place tomorrow evening?'

'Of course. I demand it of you, haha. God, I will miss you so much, Robbie.' I squeeze him tightly and we sit hugging for five or so minutes. The hug says all that needs to be said.

'I could not be happier for you. Go and get your man, Robbie, and never look back. Just don't forget me,' Ali chuckles, his eyes filling with tears but bravely fought back. Seeing his emotion stirs my own but I jump to my feet to shake them off.

'Oh, the job. My God, I am so sorry, Ali. You helped me get that job and now I have let Pak Karma down.' I feel ungrateful for the opportunity I was given to set up a life of my own in Bali.

'Pak Karma is so laid back, Robbie. He will be perfectly fine. Don't worry. Just focus on you now,' Ali tenderly says. I walk to the bedroom door to leave, and notice Ali turn his back and wipe away his tears.

'I can never repay you enough, Ali. I love you, man,' I run up behind Ali, throw my arms around him and squeeze him tightly. His body relaxes into mine. I know our time together is once again coming to an end.

Chapter Twenty-Nine

Jumping off the back of the motorcycle taxi at my room, I am greeted by Richie's children who are eager to play ball. Wayan is in the garden harvesting avocado and gives me a wave. I am so fond of these people. I do not have the heart to tell them I am leaving so soon. I throw the ball for the children to catch before chasing after them. Their giggles fill the air and draw Richie from the house.

'Hey, Robbie. You look well, sir. Will you join us for dinner later?'

'That would be great, Richie, but I have to Skype my parents. Maybe next time,' I reply. I feel guilty for lying but I am not ready to say goodbye.

Stood in my room alone, I look around at my things. Thirty years on this Earth and I have a sole suitcase to show for it. Prematurely, I pack my case ready for the start of something special in just two days. Despite Ali's offer of explaining to Pak Karma, I decide that it would be more respectful to explain to my boss in person my reasons for my sudden departure, though of course only the selective truth.

Lying down on the bed, my mind begins to race with some unanswered questions and anxieties. I have never been more certain about my love for another person, yet the situation surrounding our relationship troubles me somewhat. I feel guilt knowing that Rifqi is about to break Nadia's heart. I feel selfish that he is abandoning his family in order to be with me. Will he come to resent me in years to come when the reality of missing his family finally strikes? One thing that is clear is since my arrival in Bali, I have developed a sense of maturity that enables me to be more accepting of the unknown. When I was with Max, I was obsessed with certainty. I needed to know the details of everything: each holiday, each outing, each future event. I recognise now it came from my own insecurity in our relationship. I knew Max was playing about and a part of me wondered *when* I would lose him. I tried to be laid back, knowing my behaviour was probably pushing him further away, but the unknowns of life with him caused me severe anxiety. Although now the residues remain to some extent, the uncertainty with Rifqi fills me with excitement. Location is not important. It is all about the person I will be with. And if there are new and challenging things ahead to face, I know we will do that standing together. Only now do I understand that when I was in a relationship with Max, I actually felt alone. My eyes feel heavy, a result of little sleep last night.

I wake before sunrise. With the exception of the sounds of a few reptilian friends on the exterior walls, it is silent. Cowardly, I decide to slip out before Richie and his family wake. Despite my new found maturity, I have never enjoyed goodbyes and I hope that this is maybe just a "see you later". Standing on the roadside waiting for a cab to hail, I shiver. I am unsure if it is cooler dusk air or nerves. The early drive to the downtown avoids the frustrating snail trail traffic. Arriving at Ali's apartment, I quietly open the door and noticing Chai's shoes on the entrance mat, I decide to just leave my bag in the hallway to avoid waking them and head straight for the office, grabbing a coffee to go on the way. Surprisingly, Pak Karma is already at his desk as the sun now begins her slow climb. A slow double knock on his office door startles him from his morning donut. The thick black hair on his upper lip is dusted in sugar.

'Selamat Pagi, Mr Robbie. I am impressed to see you so early.'

'Sir, there is something I need to tell you. I... well, the thing is...' I continue to stutter.

'Mr Robbie, I understand. You leaving right? Balinese people can sense these kind of things. We are very spiritual people. Come, sit please,' he signals to the comfy, yet worn sofa in the reception area. 'First time see you, I feel your troubled soul. You lost I think. Today, you seem... how to say? Ah... found! Whatever has changed, you just go for it. Life is more important than work,' he concludes. It is the first time I have actually truly listened to him without being preoccupied with the creature that rests above his top lip. *Ah, I will miss that moustache and the way it wiggles as he speaks.* 'Will you stay to say goodbye to the others? I know Richie will miss you,' Pak Karma asks.

'I think it's best I just go now, sir. I don't like to make a fuss. Maybe sometime I will be back in Bali. The country and the people will always hold a special place in my heart.' With my closing speech complete, I leave and step out into the street, and laugh at what has probably been my briefest period of employment to date. I imagine my mother's scolding glare, judging me, but my thoughts are disrupted by a text from Ali. He will collect me late afternoon for "a special Balinese farewell".

Whilst I wait for Ali, I decide to spend a few hours in Kuta – a hustling playground for mainly Australian tourists. The short taxi ride ends just outside one of the many temples that sits nestled between night bars, fusion eateries and trendy coffee bars: memories of Ancient Civilisation co-existing among Modern Living. It is not difficult to stumble upon these mystic places of worship as Bali is home to more than 10,000 religious compounds. In fact, Ali claims that there are actually more temples than homes in Bali. Though strictly speaking, many temples are really shrines. For me, despite my lack of religious convictions, something spiritual does stir inside me whenever I visit one of the many Hindu temples scattered throughout the far-flung corners of the islands. Each one is unique and either facing towards the mountains, the sea or towards sunrise.

Stood outside the entrance of the temple, I am intimidated by the twin Dvarapala guardians. Their intricate details are carved meticulously out of the andesite stone, and are blackened and weathered by years of history. Each protector is wrapped in the traditional black and white gingham sarong. The fearsome asura giants stand proud, each armed with their gadha mace weapon. At their feet lie the daily offerings from the local worshippers. Small banana leaf trays housing beautiful flowers are accompanied by an array of food and drink items, including an ice coffee and a luminous soft drink.

One of the beautifully carved doors is pushed open so I step through the narrow opening and into the peaceful oasis. As usual, the temple is deserted and silent apart from the slight distraction of the traffic outside. The sound of trickling water somewhere ahead is soothing and I gravitate towards it. Along the perimeter wall, water flows from the remains of what appear to have been elephant heads and into a stone pool below. The stone is covered in dense green moss. I consider the number of people who have stood in this very spot during the incredible history of this place.

I meander around the compound, wondering if I will ever have the opportunity to return to this fascinating island. Rifqi will surely be running scared once we leave: escaping the judgement of his family, his people and religion. Yet, Indonesia is his home. I start to panic at the thought of pulling Rifqi from his homeland. I suddenly feel light headed and stumble on the uneven surface; the lack of breakfast is taking its effect on me.

'Maaf bli,' an older gentleman calls. I was unaware of anyone else being in the temple. He is incredibly frail but still attempts to shuffle towards me. He looks at least 90 though it may be the impact of exposure to intense sunlight that accounts for the overly shrivelled complexion. He is bare foot and wrapped in a sarong only. His painfully thin torso is on show. He continues to speak to me in Balinese as he approaches and shares a completely toothless smile with me. His eyes are glazed and frosty due to cataracts, and so I doubt he is able to see me. He knows I am a foreigner though as he refers to me as "bule" which means white man in Indonesian. His movements are painfully slow as he raises his left arm and places his palm in the centre of my chest. He simultaneously chants words which sound like Sanskrit; this is possibly a prayer I wonder. I think he senses my years of internal anguish the remains of which linger deep inside my soul. His touch is warm and soothing, the words flowing almost musically and whilst I cannot make sense of their meaning their impact takes hold. I begin to feel more relaxed and a great sense of inner peace. It is an incredibly moving experience. I close my eyes and submerge myself in his blessings. My mind tells me that things with Rifqi are going to be just fine.

'Terimah kasih,' I say as the old man completes his recital and steps back. He now stands silent and I contemplate if he is waiting for a tip so reach for my wallet. He chuckles, shares another beaming smile and slowly walks away.

Leaving the temple, I feel incredibly peaceful and moved, though my hunger pains have not subsided so I take some time to order breakfast in the hip coffee house opposite. Sitting at the window sipping on my Javanese coffee, I stare at the temple and replay my blessing from the mysterious stranger who appeared from nowhere and then disappeared, once again, nowhere to be found. The beauty of these island dwellers will forever remain in my heart. Although brief, my second affair with the Island of Gods has changed me so much as a person and of course, has given me my prince.

I watch the world go by from my viewing platform in the coffee house. The pace is slow and easy, a far cry from London. Waves of tourists trundle past: young backpackers in need of a good shower, families in search of culture and couples on romantic retreats. I contemplate our next destination, yet my daydreams are shattered prematurely by the sudden appearance of Ali, French kissing the window in front of me before giggling as he flies in through the door. Everyone turns to look at the commotion but Ali is not one to be shamed by attention.

'Surprise! I finished work early so thought I would come and grab you early,' he shrieks.

'Calm down, you crazy fool. Why are you so bloody excited?' I joke. 'You are supposed to be devastated that I am leaving tomorrow. Anyway, how did you know where to find me?'

'I didn't. But I saw that white skin glowing from 5 miles away,' Ali laughs, before throwing both arms around me. The locals smile at his flamboyant behaviour but one straight couple sit frowning at us.

'Relax, darlings. You are in Bali now,' Ali says to them as I make a quick exit totally embarrassed. Ali follows me out giggling away. He does love a scene at times which is why I am sometimes confused about why he thinks people would not automatically think he was gay. He does not exactly attempt to dampen down his flamboyancy.

'Okay, Mr. We are going to make sure that tonight Bali woes you, and forever holds a place in your heart and mind. First stop is Matahari Resort for some breath-taking views and a sunset that will make you cry. Cocktails will be flowing, thanks to Cahyo and Denny who will join us there. Next, we are off to sample some culture with a Fire Dance show.'

'But I am not really dressed for any fancy cocktail bar,' I moan.

'Look around, Mr. In comparison to some of these travellers, you are positively over-dressed.'

Ali summons our transport for the evening in the form of a 4 x 4, complete with our very own driver. I send a quick text message to Rifqi in case the night gets lost in the bottom of a cocktail glass:

How is my handsome prince?
Looks like a crazy farewell with Ali tonight.
Can't wait for tomorrow… Always xoxo
My excitement peaks when the reply pings immediately:
Have fun. Be good.
Can't wait for tomorrow too.
12pm at the departure hall.
Destination: Laos.
I will be wearing a yellow rose haha!

'Wow, look at the size of your smile. Someone's happy!' says Ali.

'We are going to Laos,' I reply looking slightly confused as I have no knowledge of this place.

I have no idea what to expect but I do know I have never been so excited for something unknown.

Chapter Thirty

We pull up outside the incredibly stylish Matahari Resort. A number of impeccably dressed young men open the car doors for us, and escort us inside where we are greeted by Cayho and Denny, already armed with cocktails for all.

'Robbie, how can you abandon us so soon?' Denny jokes.

'I would abandon everyone too if I found a sexy prince!' Cayho replies laughing as he sips on his colourful beverage.

The sunset bar sits on the edge of a dramatic cliff top. The view is breath-taking. Angry waves crash below, providing a spectacular display. Despite the low light as the day begins to come to a close, the turquoise water provides the perfect postcard of paradise. Half a kilometre or so out to sea sits the most magnificent jewel standing proud on its own island, Tanah Lot Temple. Tanah Lot Temple is a piece of architectural genius. The top of the jagged rock formation is smothered in lush green foliage providing a perfect example of eastern delight. The offshore Rock has been shaped continuously over the years by the ocean tide since its erection as a holy place to worship the sea gods. Most of the clientele at the bar surprisingly seem more interested in their alcohol consumption rates than this unique cultural icon which fascinates me. I feel mesmerised by the temple. A greater attraction pulls me towards it.

'Will you please drink up, Mr!' demands Ali.

'Are you not drawn in by the beauty of that temple,' I ask, the spectacular religious icon reminding me of the old man at the temple.

'Are you having a spiritual moment?' jests Ali. I just grin and sip my drink to please my companions. I feel embarrassed to talk of my spiritual encounter earlier that day.

'We have grown up with the beauty of Bali, Robbie. I guess we take it for granted,' suggests Denny.

The sun accelerates her descent as the second round of cocktails and nibbles are brought to our table. The bar is popular, mainly with visiting tourists staying at the resort. White shirts highlight the burnt skin from a day of sun bathing and beach fun. The sky radiates the most dramatic cocktail of red, orange and yellow hues. It's beauty finally captivates the audience, who now all turn their stools and ooh and ahh. Each passing minute sees a change in kaleidoscope of colours. A gradient of colours provides a seductive curtain behind the religious landmark.

'At the base of the rocky island, it is believed that venomous sea snakes guard the temple from evil spirits and intruders,' explains Denny, sensing my fascination with the sea temple. I realise just how interesting Denny is and wish we could have spent more time together. He seems very cultured and intelligent. 'Tanah Lot is actually one of seven sea temples along the coast of Bali,' he expands.

'Great lesson in Balinese mythology, Denny. Now drink!' Ali demands.

I realise that Ali is actually finding my imminent departure more difficult than he has let on and so is easing the pain by distracting everyone with more drink. I feel flattered.

A crimson red wave consumes the now tiny, yellow coin that rests on the horizon for her final goodbye. Tanah Lot is now a black shadow in the distance, the peaks of the temple rising high. And then she is gone. Lost in the blackness of the night. Everyone shuffles in their chairs and return to their evening potions as the resident band begin to serenade us.

'Drink up, Robbie. We have to get to the Fire Dance show in 15 minutes.'

I throw back my drink, noticing my fuzzy head from the lack of food to accompany my poison as I jump to my feet. I am certainly more relaxed. We jump in the car and head about two miles to Jimbaran, stopping outside a cultural village that has been erected for the purpose of tourism. The sound of drums beat in the background as two beautiful local girls in traditional clothing welcome us with white hibiscus flowers that they place in our hair and around our necks. Their porcelain faces look innocent and pure as they shuffle in their sarongs to show us to our seats. The small amphitheatre is surrounded by a grass weaved fence and illuminated by the tall fire torches. A small stage stands to the front, accompanied by the musical ensemble to the side. The men sit cross legged in front of an array of musical instruments waiting to be played. Bare chested men are wrapped in the same black and white gingham of the temple guards. The drums stop suddenly and the lights dim. Despite the darkness, I can make out that around 30 or so half-naked men come onto the stage and sit on the ground in a circle. The drums and accompanying instruments start quietly in the background as the men begin to chant an almost hypnotic, trance-like rhythm as they sway. In the centre of the men, a drama unfolds involving two men and a female character. I do not know the story but I am pulled in to the show. I am not sure if it's the tight ripped torsos, the chanting or the plot, but I am hooked for the next 30 minutes.

As the show comes to a close, I feel disappointment as I longed to see more.

'What did you think?' asks Ali, a sense of pride radiating from him.

'It was… unreal, Ali. Your culture fascinates me beyond any feeling I have ever experience before. Though admittedly, I have no idea what the story was about,' I laugh.

'Well, funnily enough, it is about a handsome prince and the struggles he has to overcome in order to get the girl. Sound familiar princess, Robbie?' Ali breaks out into the most contagious laugh, and before long Denny, Cahyo and myself are laughing uncontrollably too. It is the perfect end to the perfect night and the most amazing four weeks of my life.

Chapter Thirty-One

After a very restless night on Ali's sofa (on account of Chai turning up unexpectedly late last night), I begin to drift off, only to be woken by the irritating ring tone of the alarm on my phone and the mouth-watering smells waltzing out from the kitchen. I question myself on why I could not sleep. Partly, I am apprehensive about my unknown future, yet excitement burns within. Admittedly, a sense of disappointment is also present. Bali has most definitely stolen my heart. She has bestowed awe and wonder upon me, and contributed to my personal growth into an independent man. The mystery and tranquillity of this island captivates me on so many levels, and walking away again is proving challenging. I owe her so much. She has aligned the stars and by some mystical power bequeathed Rifqi to me.

'Hey, breakfast is ready, princess,' Ali shouts down the hallway.

I spring out of bed with a definite bounce in my stride. I am going to ignore my anxieties and focus only on the positives, I tell myself. I enter the kitchen wearing only my boxers to be greeted by Ali cooking in nothing more than a pair of white briefs. 'Food always did get you out of bed at Uni!' jokes Ali. 'Nothing's changed then.'

'Stop calling me princess by the way,' I take a long pause to make Ali think he has offended me before smiling and adding, 'I take my royal duties very seriously. Where is Chai?' I ask.

'Oh he left early for work. Plus I didn't want him cramping our style. I want you all to myself for a few hours before you leave.'

My eyes feel so tired as I sip on my coffee and take a few deep inhales of the mouth-watering smells circling me.

'So how are you feeling about things? Excited? Nervous?' Ali asks as he places my bowl of soto ayam on the table in front of me.

'Not exactly cornflakes, is it?' I chuckle. Ali just glares at me. I say no more to insult the chef and start slurping on my spicy chicken soup.

'Do you always cook in your skimpy pants, Ali?' I ask, trying not to look directly at his crotch.

'Yes, it adds to the ambience of the kitchen, don't you think?' Ali sniggers playfully. 'Now answer my question, HOW ARE YOU FEELING?' he pushes.

I'm mid-way slurping on my spicy morning treat so the pause is overly long. Ali appears to be holding his breath as if concerned that I am having doubts.

'I'm excited,' I reply. 'I know I just want to be with Rifqi and I know that things will work themselves out.'

'Wow, someone has become more laid back. I like it! Everything will be great. *You* will be great. You two are made for each other. I see the way he looks at you,' Ali states assertively. I smile at these words but it's wiped from my face quickly. Ali notices the transition.

'Hey, why the sudden change? Do you have any doubts?' asks Ali.

'No, not at all. Well... not so much doubts, just concerns. It just makes me a little sad the sacrifices Rifqi is having to make in order to be with me. I know how much his family mean to him,' I reply. Ali moves his chair closer to me and grabs my hand.

'Robbie, listen to me. That beautiful, gorgeous, God of a man is besotted with you and this is *his* choice to make. You cannot carry that for him. You got your happy ending after all, just like I always told you.' Ali leans in and kisses my left cheek, and whispers, 'He is a lucky man.' Ali lingers close to my cheek and as I turn my head slightly, our eyes meet. Neither of us say a word but both of us hold the gaze. His breathing is shallow, indicating he is a little nervous. I smile and prepare to lean back but suddenly, his lips are on mine. And they linger there. Neither of us step up the intensity but the kiss is prolonged. It is comforting. My eyes are open wide. Stunned, I do not move. I notice Ali's eyes are closed. I feel somewhat confused. I lean back to break the embrace and Ali blushes before jumping to his feet, and offering up more food. I consider addressing the kiss but I do not wish to embarrass him. I am not even sure how I feel about it myself. I enjoyed it but I am not sure of its meaning. I cannot deny my fondness for Ali and there is no question he is attractive but we are like brothers. *Does Ali feel more? Do I feel more?*

I decide not to address it. Whatever just happened does not matter. I will forever cherish this friendship and forever remember the kindness Ali has shown.

I take a quick shower, throw on some jeans and a t-shirt, and double check I have my passport before Ali and I set off for the airport. The drive is silent and Ali appears distracted. I am not sure if he is over-thinking the breakfast kiss or is actually a little emotional about my impending departure. I ease the tension by turning up the radio, and singing along and before long, Ali joins in. We simultaneously turn and smile at each other. I lean back in my chair and take in the Balinese sights for the final time: every temple, every person, every coconut tree, every memory all photographed and stored for future trips down memory lane. As we pull up outside departures, Ali sighs deeply.

'I will text every day,' I smile.

'Now we both know that won't happen,' Ali states with large puppy eyes, intentionally being dramatic. 'How many times have you messaged Kimberly since you left London? We all know you are hopeless with keeping in touch.'

'Okay, I will text every week,' I laugh.

I step out of the car into the choking heat and burning rays. Ali pulls my case out of the boot of the car. 'I can't bear to say goodbye in there, Ali. Let's just say "see you later" here instead. It seems so less final,' I suggest, as I begin to feel more emotional.

Ali pulls me in for hug and whispers in my ear, 'I'm sorry about *that* kiss. I don't know what I was thinking. Just overwhelmed with you leaving I guess.' I notice he does not look at me at all. I just pull him in closer and squeeze him tightly.

'I love you, Ali. I can never repay you for the kindness that you have shown to me. I am forever in your debt,' I whisper.

Ali places both hands on my cheeks, 'Go and get your prince!' I notice his eyes drowning though no tears fall. His bottom lip quivers but he holds it together. Walking into the departures hall, I refuse to look back. I know it will make me cry if I see Ali upset. There is no denying the magnetism between us. I cannot explain it but I know it is somewhere between best friends and soul mates.

I check my watch. 11.45 am. 15 minutes until the most incredible adventure begins with Rifqi.

Chapter Thirty-Two

13.45 – No sign of or sound from Rifqi. My heart is in my mouth. Rifqi is never late. He has impeccable time management considering the laid back nature of his culture and in the short time I have known him, he has never been late. I have tried to occupy myself to distract me from the negative possibilities spinning around in my head. I have looped the perimeter of the departure hall on three occasions. I have checked every shop, every toilet, every possible corner.

I check my phone for the tenth time. No messages. No missed calls. No alerts. *He is not coming, Robbie.* Fuck off, I scream at my sub-conscious. I know Rifqi would not do this to me. *Are you sure?*

Beep beep.

The reassuring text alert from my phone instantly calms my nerves as I take a seat near the check-in counters. A massive grin consumes my face as I pull my phone from my pocket. It is from Ali.

Safe flight. Rifqi is one lucky man. Love you always. x.

The endearing message does nothing to calm the rage building inside me. I want to smash my phone on the tiled floor beneath me but I desperately try to calm myself. Three deep breaths, and my anger subsides and fear now sneaks in. I consider all the possibilities of what may have happened. Am I in the wrong place? Has he changed his mind? Did he have an accident? Did I get the time wrong? Endless questions and no answers. I repeatedly check the last text message from Rifqi. I cannot sit any longer. A feeling of nausea washes over me in waves. My palms are sweaty and sticky. I get up and lap the expansive space yet again.

15.30 – Alone. Rifqi has *still* not arrived and there is no message from him. Propped up against the wall, I force myself to stop worrying but the realisation is teasing and taunting me. It laughs in my face. I feel weak and my knees buckle sending me sliding down the wall into an emotional mess on the floor. Hands to my face, my tears flood out. The cocktail of emotions and adrenaline is too much, and I feel my gut wrench. Racing to the toilet, my vomit projects into the sink. The toilet attendant glares at me disapprovingly.

'What the fuck is your problem?' I yell. He retreats quickly and I feel ashamed.

'I'm sorry!' I call after him but it is too late; he is left like a scolded child. I look into the mirror. My eyes are red with sadness. I feel like such a fool. I know he is not coming. He has chosen his family over me. He has chosen Nadia. Every promise, every kind word and every attempt at reassuring me was nothing more than a lie. He is no different to Max. And clearly, I have learnt nothing. I believed I was stronger. More realistic. Yet, I allowed myself to once again be sucked in by charm, good looks and a fantasy. I drop my head in shame. *Why are you so weak?* My tears drop into the porcelain bowl below. Each tear represents each promise broken. They group together before escaping down the plug hole. I see my father's face staring back at me in the mirror. He looks welcoming, and I think he wants to hug me but his face changes and a disapproving look glares back. He shakes his head. My weakness angers him. I know I am hallucinating and shake my head to rid him from my thoughts.

I feel paralysed. I do not know what to do. I have nothing. I have no ticket to fly out of here and I have given up any hope of a life in Bali. Yet, a part of me still believes in Rifqi. I check my phone again in the hope that there is a perfectly sensible explanation. 16.35 – no messages, no missed calls.

I know I cannot stay hidden in the men's room much longer. Security has already come in a few times to check on the crazy white guy losing his shit. I splash my face with the cold water, though it does nothing to remove the crimson blotches. Case dragging behind me, I enter the departures hall and head for the ticket counter. The airline agent looks a little alarmed on account of my clearly emotional persona. Her eyes widen and she whispers something to her colleague.

'One ticket to London Heathrow, please,' I ask.

'Return, sir?'

'One way out of here!' I retort.

'No! Stop! Don't go. I'm here,' shouts a frantic voice from behind me.

Chapter Thirty-Three

'Ali? What the hell are you doing back here?' I yell. He looks petrified. The colour from his cheeks has drained and he has clearly been crying on the way here. I cannot deal with any more drama from Ali but suddenly, I realise he should have assumed I was already in Laos. Why would he have come to the airport now? He is physically shaking. It's scaring me. He just stares back; his bottom lip is once again quivering. His head shakes back and forth in slow motion before dropping to his chest. I know something is terribly wrong but I am frozen to my spot. I cannot bear to hear what Ali has to say. His persona alone tells me that he is not bringing good news. I try to move towards him. My legs feel heavy, slowing me down. He seems so far away. His head lifts slowly and as our eyes connect, he whispers, 'I'm so sorry. So, so, sorry.' I grab hold of his arms which hang limply to his body.

Despite not wishing to know the answer, I take a long inhale of breath and ask, 'Ali... what's happened? What's wrong? Please tell me...' The pause between my last word and Ali's first lingers. We stare deep into each other's eyes; mine are begging him to tell me. I see the pain eating him. It is not his own pain but the one he is about to impart on me. He loves me too much to wish to inflict this upon me. I sense this. I understand. But I need him to just say the words.

'Ali. God-damnit, just fucking tell me,' I scream, now feeling frantic. Ali's lips are pale and dry. He licks them moist and slowly opens his mouth. Tears precede his words.

'It's Rifqi,' he says barely audible. My chest tightens in anticipation.

'He's... he... there was accident... he's... dead.' The last word hollers out from Ali's mouth and echoes all around me. I hear the word on repeat – screeching and scraping at my ears. It amplifies with each echo. I cannot bear it. The word crushes me from the inside out. A giant fist punches through my chest cavity and strangles my heart. Every drop of love drained from it. I cannot catch my breath. Am I suffocating? I stumble forward; my legs cannot support my weight. Ali catches me just as the room darkens and I pass out.

I open my eyes but I am not at the airport. I am laying in a grass field. The sun is beating down on my face. Slowly, I sit up. I hear Rifqi laughing in the distance and I jump to my feet. Walls of dense hedge spring up around me. I am in some kind of maze. Pathways lead in every direction. I hear Rifqi giggling behind me and run in that direction. A solid wall appears and blocks my path. I change direction but no matter where I run, my path is stopped. Rifqi continues to call me but I cannot reach him. I try to scramble over the hedge but it is too high and I fall. He sounds so happy. He sounds free. I long to see his face. I knew he would not leave me here. His voice calls out ahead of me again. I sprint towards the hedge and push my way through, the tangled branches tear, and scratch at my face and arms. He is there standing in front of me. He looks just as I remembered. Smiling, of course.

'I knew you wouldn't leave me here, Rifqi,' I say.

He does not reply but the smile slowly disappears. The colour in his cheeks drains. His eyes darken; his cheeks sink. He looks to be in pain. He appears distraught. I run to him and reach out my arms but he is gone. I scream out his name like a mantra but he does not respond. My own voice echoes back at me. The green foliage dries and turns brown, and the ground beneath my feet turns to mud. My feet sink further into the earth below. It reaches my waist and I can no longer move. The force against my chest is now unbearable and I sink further and further. I fight to catch my breath as the last rays of light disappear. 'RIFQI!! RIFQI!!' I scream out.

'Robbie… Robbie,' calls Ali. My head is in his lap and he appears to be in a panic. A small crowd of spectators have gathered around us to enjoy the drama. A few airport officials are trying to be helpful. The resident doctor takes my pulse and a young nurse wipes my brow. For a moment, I feel disorientated. I cannot make the connections, but as my mind replays the past few hours, it becomes clear. Rifqi is gone.

'Let's get you back home,' Ali whispers.

Ali drives us from the airport. I am unable to support my own weight. I lay down in the back of the car. Flashes of light from the street lamps and night bars reflect in the rear windows. Ali continues to watch me in the rear view mirror. His eyes look sympathetically back at me. I know he wants to take away some of my pain but maybe he does not know how and I am not even sure there is anything he could possibly do to take away this immense agony. This is my pain alone. My head pounds from every angle. So many feelings entering and exiting in quick succession. It is difficult to make any sense of them. I sit up suddenly aware I do not know the circumstances or even how Ali knew.

'Ali... how did you find out? About Rifqi, I mean.'

'It was announced on TV,' Ali replies. Immediately, I consider the reliability of the information source. *Maybe it is a hoax?* Ali says with further clarification 'I found Wahyu's number on a name card you left in the apartment and called him. He confirmed. I'm sorry, Robbie. He was devastated. I could barely understand a word he was saying about the accident.' Ali freezes on the last word and looks back at me in the mirror. I suspect he knows what my next question will be, though I am not sure I am ready to hear just yet. A wave of sickness arrives suddenly. My stomach wrenches. It is so guttural. I desperately try to contain it but the vomit spills out. The taste is so acidic it dries my mouth instantly.

'Robbie, hold on back there, we are almost home,' Ali says sympathetically. With each beat of my heart, my head pounds. The sharp pain pierces behind my eye sockets.

We arrive at his apartment and Ali guides me to the bedroom, trying desperately to prop up my weight. My legs feel so heavy. I drop to the bed and sink deep into the mattress. Safe in the privacy of Ali's home, I scream out Rifqi's name. I feel so confused. I cannot process the infinite number of questions and emotions that bombard me. I long to see Rifqi's face right now. That smile that can heal any level of pain. I yearn to hear him say my name with that adorable accent. *He has gone, Robbie.* I flip myself over and scream into the pillow, kicking and screaming in desperation until I tire. My body is weak. I feel like I have been punched and kicked in every limb. Ali places a soothing hand on my back and tries to calm me. Slowly, his touch eases my anger and I give up. I lay still on the bed. Silent. No more tears come. I have run dry. Now would be a good time to know what happened. I am calm and collected, or at least I try to tell myself that I am.

'Ali, what happened? I need to know.'

'Robbie. He didn't leave you at the airport. He was trying to reach you.' Ali smiles knowing these words will offer some comfort, even if only short-lived.

'Rifqi was travelling on his motorbike at high speed, most likely to the airport,' Ali suggests.

'And... what happened?' I ask nervously, knowing that I do not wish to hear the ending.

'He collided with another bike and was flung across the road. He died instantly. I am so sorry, Robbie.' Ali begins to cry once again.

'Did the other rider explain how it happened? Rifqi was such a good rider. He would never crash into another bike,' I reply defensively.

'The other motorist didn't stop, Robbie. The police say he fled the scene.'

We sit silently for a moment pondering these words. My mind races with thoughts and theories, some without any logic. I desperately try to piece together the events. Rifqi must have told his family and Nadia that he could not go through with the wedding. Maybe there was an argument, and Rifqi told them he was gay and about our plans. No doubt, everyone tried to make him see sense. To turn away from the dark side. Threats of being expelled from the family and burning in hell would have taken up so much time. He must have made a quick exit and been speeding to avoid missing the flight to Bali. He was coming for me. He didn't abandon me. He is not like Max. He really is my White Knight. *Was. He is gone, Robbie, remember?* He *was* my White Knight. But he has abandoned me now. Left me here alone to face the music. How will I explain this to his family? *Amat must be furious.* Amat! *The other rider fled the scene.* Did Amat chase after his brother and in his haste cause the accident? Would a family go that far to protect Rifqi's dirty secret? I feel so confused. Ali just sits looking at me but I cannot express my thoughts. They seem insane. Would a brother really kill his sibling? I know I am exhausted and not being logical. The tension in my body eases and I begin to slowly relax. My eyes feel so heavy as Ali strokes my hair and I begin to feel myself drifting off.

The sudden feeling of drowning wakes me suddenly. The room is pitch black. Hours must have passed. Ali has finally left my side. The silence of the apartment is deafening. For a brief moment, I am numb. I have no feelings and no memory. I feel quite disorientated as I sit up in the bed. I hear a sound coming from another room and assume it is Rifqi. I imagine him walking back into the bedroom wrapped in a white towel. His perked pecs teasing me with inappropriate thoughts. I picture that caramel skin beneath my palms and imagine his lips on mine. The sweet taste lingers on my tongue. I close my eyes and desperately try to make it a reality but he does not come. The absoluteness of his absence returns for another fight. She throws repeated punches in my face and abdomen, taking the wind from me. But this time she goes too far, and despite my weakness, my fury returns and I lash out at my imaginary intruder. A rage so raw rips out from me. It has no focus for attack; Rifqi, his family, his narrow-minded culture, his religion, Amat, Nadia. In fact, I want to take on the world right now. My outrage boils my blood and I lash out at the objects in front of me, sending them flying to all four corners of the room. Glass shatters around the bed bringing Ali darting into the room in a panic.

The sight of his face, looking on at me empathetically, makes me crumble and despair sets in once more. I scream out for Rifqi. I believe that if I say his name enough times and loud enough, he can return. I cannot comprehend that he has gone. I cannot process it. It makes no sense to me.

'I need to see him, Ali. I need to see him resting peacefully. I want to say goodbye,' I cry.

'Robbie. It's too late,' Ali whispers, dropping his head to avoid looking me in the eye. 'In keeping with the Muslim religion, Rifqi has already been buried. He's gone, Robbie.'

Ali's words pierce my heart repeatedly. The sharp pain is almost unbearable to withstand. Ali grabs me in his arms and I fall into his chest. He rocks me side to side as I whimper and cry. I feel so alone. So vulnerable. So lost. It is then I am sure I hear Rifqi's voice calling my name gently. The sound is healing. My prince didn't abandon me. He is still waiting for me. Just in a different place than planned.

Epilogue

Standing at the foot of the grave, a shiver runs along my spine. Ali rests a hand on my shoulder and gives a little reassuring squeeze. I feel truly blessed to have such a supportive person in my life. For the past six months, Ali has wiped my tears, listened to my cries, ensured I ate and drank, and slowly helped me to get back on to my feet. He has the magical balance between support and patience, kindness and encouragement. Night after night, he has sat with me until I drift off to sleep and laid next to me when I have woken in the middle of the night screaming out Rifqi's name.

I take a few steps forward, leaving Ali to retreat to the shelter of the tree. My hands shake as I lower the yellow roses and place them next to the headstone. I cannot bring myself to read his name. I know it his resting place but I cannot bear to see his name. The grave has been well kept as expected. It sits in a private section of the graveyard, reserved for those of noble background. The impressive black granite headstone casts a shadow where Rifqi sleeps. I kneel down and touch the ground, and close my eyes. I long to imagine I am resting my hand on his chest. 'I'm so sorry, Rifqi. I should never have allowed this to happen. Your destiny was never with me. Forgive me.' Two tears drop onto the soil below. I try to keep my composure. Today's visit is about letting go and beginning the process of moving on. I lean forward and kiss the ground, and whisper, 'Goodnight, my handsome prince. In another lifetime, I hope to see you again. I will love you always.'

The wind whistles around me, the sound of the branches swaying behind me. I hear Rifqi whisper back, 'Miss me, but let me go.' I lift my head suddenly, praying he will be stood behind me. I turn, but only Ali walks towards me, smiling.